H<small>IS</small> <small>BREATH WAS WARM ON HER NECK AS</small> he moved behind her. She was ready to scream from the intensity of the desire mounting in her body.

"What do you want, April?" Jack whispered hoarsely.

Her only response, the only one she was capable of, was a shiver that ran the length of her body. She heard the soft rustle of fabric, then a click, and the office was bathed in moonlight.

"Do you want me to touch you, *mi tesoro*?" Jack's breath was warm on the skin behind her ear. She nodded. "Do you know you affect me like no other woman? I'm intrigued by your control, fascinated by your sensuality. . . ."

April thought she'd go mad from the mixture of wonder and need that laced his rough tone.

Wrapping his arms around her waist, he nuzzled her neck, reveling in every breath, every sigh. He took another deep breath of her sweet scent, the hint of muskiness from her skin burning his senses.

"Touch me," she begged softly.

He bit his inner cheek, struggling for control. "If I do, I won't stop. Not until every inch of your skin knows the feel of me."

"Yes. . . ."

WHAT ARE *LOVESWEPT* ROMANCES?

They are stories of true romance and touching emotion. We believe those two very important ingredients are constants in our highly sensual and very believable stories in the LOVESWEPT *line. Our goal is to give you, the reader, stories of consistently high quality that may sometimes make you laugh, sometimes make you cry, but are always fresh and creative and contain many delightful surprises within their pages.*

Most romance fans read an enormous number of books. Those they truly love, they keep. Others may be traded with friends and soon forgotten. We hope that each LOVESWEPT *romance will be a treasure—a "keeper." We will always try to publish*

LOVE STORIES YOU'LL NEVER FORGET
BY AUTHORS YOU'LL ALWAYS REMEMBER

The Editors

TANGO IN PARADISE

DONNA KAUFFMAN

BANTAM BOOKS
NEW YORK · TORONTO · LONDON · SYDNEY · AUCKLAND

TANGO IN PARADISE

A Bantam Book / June 1994

If you would be interested in receiving protective vinyl covers for your
Loveswept books, please write to this address for information:

Loveswept
Bantam Books
P.O. Box 985
Hicksville, NY 11802

ISBN 0-553-44380-1

Published simultaneously in the United States and Canada

PRINTED IN THE UNITED STATES OF AMERICA

OPM   0 9 8 7 6 5 4 3 2 1

To Carmen—for always being there.
Your friendship is priceless.

ONE

If there was a place worse than hell, then that's where her day was headed.

"What do you mean they're *both* gone?" April Morgan asked into the cellular phone as she stepped through the side door of Paradise Cove into the bright Mexican sunshine. It wasn't even nine A.M., and the resort was already blanketed with a thick layer of humidity that the typically windy conditions did little to disperse.

April sighed in resignation as her assistant relayed the bad news. She paused by the stuccoed pillars that framed the main entrance. "Carmen, don't tell me I've lost my head bartender and my *only* staff photographer"—April shifted the folders in her left arm to her right, glanced at her watch,

then shifted everything back, barely missing a beat—
"less than five hours before the wedding rehearsal
for Senator Smithson's only daughter. Do you know
why?"

April exhaled a long, frustrated breath through
clenched teeth as Carmen explained that Steve and
Bernardo had decided, after sharing a bottle of
wine, that they had a life together and wanted to
explore the possibilities.

"All this from a bottle of Chianti? Couldn't
they have 'explored the possibilities' *after* the ceremony?" The question was academic, as Carmen went on to explain that the two had cleared
out their belongings and apparently left the resort
for good.

Irritated as she was by their untimely departure, April pushed the why's and how's out of her
mind and focused her attention on getting replace-
ments.

"Find Paolo for me and tell him he'll have to
work the bar this afternoon after all. Then see if
you can get through to Club Med and beg, borrow,
or steal us a photographer. Give them whatever
they want. I doubt they'll be able to get someone
here by this afternoon, but tomorrow for the wedding will do. Beep me when you get an answer."

April clicked off, tucked the phone into the
side pocket of her floral skirt, then stared unseeing
across the resort compound as she tried and failed

to come up with a backup plan in case Carmen didn't succeed.

Building a resort in the middle of nowhere hadn't been her intention when she'd fled Washington for the privacy of her grandfather's small charter-fishing service ten years ago. If he were still alive, she was sure he'd appreciate the irony of how the very remoteness of the southern coastal area she'd once insisted would be the solution to all her problems was now the source of so many new ones. Yet, it was his advice that had enabled her to deal with so many of them. "April Marie," he'd said, "you want somethin' bad enough, you gotta go and get it. It sure as hell ain't gonna come to you."

She looked around at what she'd built on that advice and had to smile. She heard that gravelly voice now as clearly as if he were standing beside her. "That's all fine and well, Gramps," she said quietly into air fragrant with the blossoms of the bougainvillea he'd loved. "I just wished you'd added a few words of wisdom on how I'm supposed to go and get something that isn't around to be got."

April smiled and nodded to a few guests who stepped out onto the terraced entrance. Her smile faded when she heard the sounds of an escalating argument in the side parking lot.

Both voices were masculine. One spoke the musical tones of the Spanish dialect native to the villagers who made up most of the Cove's work force. The other voice was deeper, rougher, definitely not as polite, and came through in rather voluble English.

"Now what?" April usually let her staff handle the smaller crises, but she wanted to handle this herself, even though her agenda already read like the to-do list for reforming a third world country. Maybe it was the proverbial last straw. More likely, she just couldn't resist the temptation to tackle a problem she had an actual chance at solving.

Rounding one of the large stone pillars that supported the roof of the covered guest lot, April spied the two men. One she immediately recognized as Miguel, a longtime employee and her best bellman.

The other man, apparently a newly arrived guest, stopped her in her tracks.

He was substantially taller than Miguel, and his hair was a windblown mass of brown waves. The rolled-up sleeves of his blue and white striped cotton shirt revealed muscular forearms, and riding low on his hips were jeans so old they had long ago formed a permanent, perfect fit to his muscular thighs and backside. Goodness, she thought as she ran her gaze over him again, even from a distance he made quite an imposing figure.

She tore her gaze away—surprised at her reluctance to do so—and focused on the object of a tug-of-war between her smiling, but adamant, bellman and her much larger, and definitely not smiling, new guest. Banged up and not quite as shiny, the silver case still looked a lot like the one that Steve, her absent photographer, had always packed his camera equipment in.

No, she thought, this would be too good to be true. She never got anything without suffering for it.

You want somethin' bad enough, you gotta go and get it. Her grandfather's words rang in her ears. She smiled and headed across the lot. "Right on, Gramps."

As she drew closer to her new guest, several things struck her all at once. He had a roguish-looking day's growth of beard, maybe two days' worth, and his hair was actually lighter than she'd thought, streaked liberally with blond. Those wind-blown strands, as well as his jeans and shirt, had so much road dust on them she had to wonder if he'd rolled to the resort.

Neither man heard her approach and she took a quick glance into the battered Jeep that was parked beside the men. On the backseat was a canvas duffel bag and a beat-up nylon bag with what looked like a camera strap hanging out of the unzipped top. Bingo!

She glanced at her guest again. So what if he was a far cry from the typical well-groomed, heavy-walleted guest who frequented Paradise Cove? If that silver case contained the equipment she hoped it did, he could be wearing a loincloth and still be the best thing she'd ever seen.

Resisting that mental picture, she cleared her throat. When that didn't get either of the men's attention, she placed her hand on the guest's arm. His skin was hot and gritty and she could feel the pulse of the veins that stood out in stark relief. She quickly dropped her hand. "Excuse me, maybe I can be of some help here?"

He turned to her, ran a quick, appraising look over her short, slender body that left her feeling as though she'd just been frisked, then turned back to her bellman without comment. She was just about to step in again, a bit more forcefully this time, when he spoke.

"If you can make this guy stop grinning and nodding long enough to let go of my camera case, then the answer is yes."

His deep voice sounded like gravel baked in the sun—hot, dusty, and a bit rough. April ignored his less than gracious behavior. She'd dealt with far worse in her thirty-two years. She smoothly cut in between the men and spoke to Miguel rapidly in the local Spanish dialect. The bellman nodded with a polite smile and immediately let go of the silver case. "Thank you, Miguel," she finished. "Could you please get us a cart?"

Only after the bellman turned away did she face

her guest, a pleasant smile carved on her face. If she expected gratitude, one look at his expression told her she'd have a long wait. She'd apparently counted her blessings a bit prematurely. "Cooperative" wasn't the first word that came to mind when she looked into his eyes. Or the second.

Irritation. Fatigue. Resignation at having to deal with yet another unwanted obstacle. Those were the things she saw as she gazed up into those startling light green depths.

"Look, miss, I appreciate you calling off the trained seal. And thanks, but I don't need a cart. I've lugged these bags thousands of miles; I think I can make it to the lobby." As if to prove his point, he hoisted the nylon tote on one shoulder, looping the long strap over his head, and shifted it across his broad chest. He then hefted the duffel bag out of the back of the Jeep before turning back to face her.

April pasted on her the-guest-is-always-right smile. She'd long ago learned it was the only way to deal with irascible guests and keep her sanity.

His use of the words "camera case" should have made the chore easier. But his quick, piercing assessment of her—which he'd made clear she'd failed miserably—still stuck under her skin like an annoying splinter. That confused her. She'd stopped trying to prove herself a long time ago, having come to believe that success spoke louder than any number of well-chosen words.

And the last thing she wanted was for him to respond to her as a woman. All she needed from him was a quick resume, and some information on how well he could handle his equipment.

"I know I look a bit rough for the wear." The corner of his mouth curled, slightly relieving the harshness of his bristled jaw. "If I promise you I clean up real good, would you point me in the direction of the lobby? I'd be eternally grateful."

Instead of tired frustration, his weary voice held what sounded like a trace of amusement. April blinked twice before she realized she had been assessing him every bit as closely as he had her.

Only she'd taken a bit longer.

"Ah, certainly." She squared her shoulders, as if it would give her instant command of the situation, but she still had to force her gaze away from him. "Just this way." She headed back around the side path. Maybe with a bit of distance she could manage more scintillating conversation. "I take it you had a rough trip?"

He caught up with her in a few strides, which surprised her, considering how worn-out he looked. Glancing down at her, he answered in a dry tone. "In the last sixteen hours, I've reduced my necessary-for-survival list to a cold beer, a hot shower, and about two days of uninterrupted sleep."

By the time they reached the entrance to the resort, April was almost trotting to keep up with his long-legged gait. The man had at least a foot on her in height, all apparently from the waist down.

He stopped just inside the open doorway, and she took a split second too long noticing. She barely avoided ramming into him, and had to balance her hands against his back to steady herself. He turned swiftly at her touch, managing to tangle her bracelets in the straps hanging from his shoulder and draped across his chest.

"I'm sorry, I seem to be stuck." April tried to pull her hands out, but the thin silver bracelets only seemed to tangle more tightly with her efforts.

"Whoa, slow down for a minute."

He set down the silver case on the tiled floor, and when he straightened, her nose was a mere inch from the dark hair curling damply above the opened front buttons of his shirt. He grasped her wrists and tried to tug them free. His skin was warm and rough, his hands so large her wrists looked like fragile twigs in comparison. When tugging didn't work, he let go of her wrists and gripped the bracelets.

"Pull out."

His rough voice jerked her gaze upward. She stared at him dumbly. A tiny electric current started at his touch on her wrists, singed a path along her arm to her shoulder, and ended at the sensitive spot at the center of her nape, which tingled as he gazed down at her. "Pull out of what?"

A smile—one of distinct masculine recognition—crossed his face. Her mind went blank, her heart pounded. Lord, just a hint of white teeth and she felt as if he'd hot-wired her pulse.

She instinctively tried to tug her hands away from him, and yanked them right out of her bracelets.

"These," he responded, his smile widening as he held up the sterling circles. When she made no move to take them, he lifted her hand and started to slide them back on.

"Don't. I mean, I can do that." She pulled out of his grasp and slid the bangles back on, wishing she could regain her wits as easily.

She gestured toward the groupings of rattan furniture scattered around the tiled lobby. "Why don't you have a seat and I'll get you checked in." She turned back to face him. "I assume you have reservations, Mr . . . ?"

"Tango. Jack Tango." His crooked smile was boyishly endearing. "As for reservations, if you mean about staying here, yes. But since I didn't have the option of choosing where I was sent, I'll just have to live with it." The irritation underlying his words was impossible to miss. "Thanks again for your help, but I can take it from here."

It didn't take a genius to figure out that he wanted to get rid of her. As if to prove her assumption, he nodded and turned to go. April noticed the silver case still sitting on the floor next to her feet. "Ah, Mr. Tango? Wait a minute."

He paused, hung his head briefly, then slowly turned. "Listen, I really appreciate everything. I'm sorry if I seem rude, it's just that it's been a rough day." He broke off, arched his neck and rolled his shoulders as if working the kinks out, then let out a humorless laugh.

"Hell, who am I kidding? I've had a year of rough days. Now Franklin sends me down here to this dusty, godforsaken scrap of real estate. The only vehicle I could find should be enshrined in a museum . . ." He tilted his head forward to look directly at her. "I'm supposed to be relaxing. Can you believe that? Vacations."

He made the last word sound like an obscenity. April felt sorry for his exhaustion, but couldn't help wondering why he was here. Who was Franklin? It hadn't taken long to figure out that Jack Tango wasn't the type of man to take orders or do anything he didn't want to. She'd kill for five minutes with this Franklin, just to find out how he'd persuaded Mr. Tango to do anything.

She stooped and retrieved his case. "You forgot your camera case."

He uttered a choice expletive and then, more

loudly, said, "I must be worse off than I thought."

She recalled how reluctant he'd been to relinquish his gear to Miguel. Obviously he took photography very seriously. That thought sent a surge of renewed hope racing through her.

"No problem," she assured him. "I'm sorry, but in the shuffle, I neglected to introduce myself. I'm April Morgan, CEO of Paradise Cove." Hoping to score a few points for her cause, she flashed her best professional smile and said, "If you'll let me help you, I can get your hand wrapped around a cold beer in record time."

Jack's eyes widened. She was all of five-foot-nothing, with surprising curves, wild curly hair, and a smile that made him alter his survival list from a hot shower to a cold one. And she had just blithely claimed to be in charge of a multimillion-dollar resort.

He must be as burned-out as his colleagues had finally churned up the guts to tell him he was. Because damned if he didn't believe her.

"Maybe vacations aren't such a bad thing after all." Had he really just said that? He'd fought like hell over taking a leave of absence. And pushing that damned Jeep under a sun that went on full-broil just minutes after sunrise had only made him sorry he hadn't fought harder for an assignment instead.

"Have a seat over there," she said. "I'll be right

back with your key." She flashed another brilliant smile, but didn't wait for an answer.

Jack shrugged and accepted defeat for the first time that day. He was surprised that he didn't mind it so much if it meant he might get to see that smile again.

He headed toward a cluster of benches, then heaped his gear on one and sat on another. This way he didn't have to look at the floral print on the cushions. The bright colors made his eyes hurt.

The sexy, raven-haired woman arranging his stay presented a far more delectable picture.

Uh-uh, Tango, he silently warned himself. He was here for R&R, and neither of those *R*'s stood for relationships. Physical or otherwise. Still, it couldn't hurt to look and lust a little. He certainly had no intentions of sating that lust.

He allowed his mind to indulge in a few choice scenarios as he watched her walk back toward him, the filmy material of her flowery skirt and yellow blouse clinging to and outlining every curve of her body.

She stopped in front of him, smiling, dangling his room key as if it were a talisman that would open doors of delight. All he had to do was reach out and . . .

"Are you all right?" Her eyes widened. "Stay here; your reservation is for one of our private bungalows. I'll get one of our golf carts to take you there."

Her voice had grown deeper, huskier—but with concern, not desire. That realization jolted him out of his hormone-induced stupor. He hadn't ogled anyone like a teenager since ... well, since he'd been a teenager. If that weren't bad enough, he was more turned on than he'd been in recent memory—and she thought he was physically ill!

Embarrassed, he immediately pulled himself to his feet and, gritting his teeth against the stiffening muscles in his lower back, he hefted his gear. "That won't be necessary. I can walk."

Her expression left no doubt that she didn't think he could make it out of the lobby, much less to the long-awaited wonders of his very own bungalow. He blamed the heat and the lack of sleep for reducing him to feeling the need to prove he was a man—proof right there that he was no longer capable of rational thought. But he trudged past her toward the closest exit anyway, determined to make it to the bungalow or die trying.

It proved to be a tougher campaign than he'd thought.

They stepped out onto a terraced set of stone steps that led down to a startling blue pool of water. The sun glinted directly off the sparkling surface, making Jack wince and grab for his sunglasses. Slipping the black shades onto the bridge of his nose, he skirted the steps and headed toward the path that cut through the trees just past the pool.

April watched him saunter off, sorely tempted to let him wander off by himself. He'd get lost before he ever found the guest bungalows. They were nestled at the rear of the resort. In the opposite direction.

But the silver equipment case swinging in his hand made her hurry to catch up. "You're going the wrong way," she called out. "This is the way to the employee bungalows. Guest cottages are that way."

He paused, then stopped. He set down the silver case, shifted the duffel to his other shoulder, picked up the case, and walked back to her. April found herself admiring the way he moved, wondering what he'd look like freshly shaven with a smile on his face, wishing he didn't have those dark sunglasses on so she could see his intriguing eyes. . . .

Yanking her thoughts back to her present personnel problem, she directed her gaze to the silver case. It was on the tip of her tongue to simply explain her situation and hope for the best. She just wasn't sure how to explain it without sounding like a total idiot.

"Your bungalow is number fourteen," she said. "It's down this path. Last one on the left." Maybe it would be better to approach him with her request after he'd showered and changed, she decided. She held out what looked like a plastic credit card. "Your key."

Jack watched a myriad of expressions flicker across her face as if she was struggling with some important matter. Her exotic almond-shaped eyes were a warm shade of brown. Her sensually full bottom lip all but begged him to discover if her mouth tasted as succulent as it looked. Her husky voice was still arousing his body, which, considering what he'd been through today, should have been dead. And it had been, until about fifteen minutes ago. He wondered what she was thinking about.

Take the key and get out of here, Tango, he lectured himself. Instead he tilted his head in the direction of his bungalow. "I don't seem to have a free hand. Would you mind?" Her gaze narrowed warily. "After all, you've come this far."

April studied him. Had he placed a specific emphasis on his last sentence? It had been over ten years, but she was still sensitive to sexual innuendo. And she couldn't deny that his visual inventory of her had left her feeling unusually vulnerable. But there was still the matter of finding a photographer. Unless she wanted a complete disaster on her hands over the next twenty-four hours, she had to persuade Mr. Tango to help her out.

Besides, he was certainly in no shape to put any moves on her. "Only if you'll let me carry something heavier than this key the rest of the way."

"Deal." He peeled off the strap of the small nylon bag and handed it to her. He swept his arm in front of him. "After you."

And then he smiled.

April knew right then that Jack Tango was far from being a problem she could easily solve.

And that he would be anything but the simple solution to hers.

TWO

April hurried up the few steps to the tiny bungalow and had barely opened the door before Jack pushed past her. He tossed his sunglasses on the bar, then dropped onto the small couch, letting his duffel bag slide off his arm. It tilted over, wadded-up clothing spilling onto the woven rug covering the cushions.

"Ahhh. Air-conditioning." His voice was almost reverent in appreciation. "Second-best invention known to man."

The question was out before she could stop it. "What's the first? Electric blankets?"

His light-eyed gaze pinned her where she stood. She felt like a butterfly caught against a velvet board.

"Right now the need for artificial heat is the last thing on my mind."

April gulped. "Yes, well . . . let me show you where everything is and I'll be on my way. I'm sure you want a shower. There should be cold—"

"Aren't you still curious about what's first?"

April made a valiant effort to give him her professional smile. "Let me guess," she said brightly. "Cold beer?" Not letting him answer, she continued. "Aside from a well-stocked kitchen and bar, the bungalow comes equipped with two phones: one by the couch and one in the bedroom."

"That's it."

"What?"

"The number one thing. Room service. Everything you desire is at the touch of your fingertips— and you never need to leave the bedroom."

She gauged the tired grin on his face. She wasn't about to take that dangerous piece of bait. "Well, if you desire something that's not already here," she said as matter-of-factly as possible, "just call the front desk and they'll have it here before you finish unpacking."

Jack arched a doubtful brow and looked pointedly at his duffel bag and the scattered clothes.

April couldn't help but laugh. "Okay, maybe even we aren't that quick. You'll probably have time for a shower." Her smile grew a bit uncertain as Jack rose slowly and took a step toward her. Time to leave. "I, uh, have to get back." He took another step. "I'm really very busy." She reached the open doorway. "If you have any questions I'm sure the room steward or Dominguez, our concierge, can answer them."

"Thanks," he responded. "I'll be sure to make a list."

April's concern about just what—or who—might be on that list diminished as he drew nearer. On close inspection, his eyes looked like light green marbles caught in red spiderwebs. His voice was a bit scratchy and when he smiled—that little one that turned his lips up a little at one corner—it was easy to forget the predatory gaze he'd raked over her not moments ago. She breathed a quick sigh of relief. "You're welcome. I hope you enjoy your stay."

She had descended to the second step when she realized she hadn't even approached the subject of her need for his services. At this point, and given his fatigue, she could hardly just blurt out a casual, "Oh, by the way, if you're not doing anything later, would you mind shooting a wedding rehearsal for a senator's daughter. . . ."

But she couldn't leave without at least trying to set things up to her advantage for later.

She turned back to find him standing in the open doorway.

"Is there something else?"

She stared up at him. How could someone so tired still look so . . . virile? "No, not really." *Chicken.* She drew in a quick breath. "I know you'd like to rest. But, if you'd like, I can have the desk ring you in time for the late lunch seating."

Jack didn't know whether to laugh or groan. She just didn't give up. He finally hung his head in silent defeat. Why didn't she just leave? But for that matter, why had he followed her to the door? He needed sleep. Craved it. And now he was finally standing less than ten feet away from his entire list of survival necessities.

So why was he actually giving serious thought to her invitation?

At that moment his body decided to take matters into its own hands, and he felt his knees start to sway. Crossing his arms over his chest, he leaned his shoulder against the door frame to cover his rapidly evaporating strength. Macho theatrics right to the end, he thought. "Sorry, but I don't plan on being conscious for at least twenty-four hours."

Surprisingly, her polished smile faltered a bit. For a brief second true disappointment shone in her eyes. He didn't want it to, but that small ripple in her seemingly unflappable cool bothered him. Aw, hell. Locking one knee and crossing his ankles to bolster himself, he added, "But I'm sure by tomorrow morning I'll be starving. How about breakfast? Say, around nine?"

"Of course. That'll be fine." She nodded nicely enough, but the smile didn't come back.

For some ridiculous reason he was too tired to analyze, he didn't want her to leave without one. Even that fakey CEO smile would do. Then he could let her go. "Ms. Morgan?"

She turned back, resting one hand on the stair railing. "Yes?" The sunlight filtered through the thin fabric of her yellow blouse and outlined the gentle curve of one side of her waist and the fullness of a breast. "Is there something else?"

A number of responses came to mind, but all of them required energy, and he was presently using all of his just to breathe and stay upright. But he couldn't ignore the sense that he'd disappointed her somehow. "Was there any particular reason you wanted me to eat lunch?"

She started, obviously caught off guard. "Why do you ask?"

"You just seemed so . . . I don't know." He took a deep breath and pushed away from the door frame, paused for a moment, then dragged a hand through his hair. "I just got the feeling you were . . . disappointed that I wanted to sleep the day away. Since I doubt you'll miss my sterling personality, it must be something else. Does the resort have some policy that all guests attend lunch?"

It was a weak attempt at humor, but her expression remained one of polite restraint as she shook her head. Yet his trained eye didn't miss the subtle motion of her throat muscles flexing as she swallowed.

Lord, he thought, momentarily spellbound, the camera would love her. His fingers itched to grab his favorite Nikon and run off a roll or two.

As if she'd read his mind, her gaze strayed into the bungalow behind him, stopping at his equipment bags. He looked at them, too, then back at her.

Uh-oh. She wanted something from him, and based on the equipment she'd chosen to look at, it wasn't his body—though at the moment he could hardly blame her. Still, it irritated him that he'd completely misread the signals.

All traces of the teasing tone he'd tried earlier disappeared. "Let me guess, you want something from me and I bet it has nothing to do with proper nutrition." She looked guiltier than sin on Sunday, but he felt a grudging respect when she lifted her chin a notch.

"Actually, there is something—"

"Sorry. No dice." His voice hardened a bit. He felt like such a sucker. "I came here to get away from work for a while."

April held his gaze. She should have known finding a photographer literally on her doorstep was too good to be true. But there was no point in backing off now. "I realize how tired you are, and if it weren't so important I'd never ask for help from a guest, but—"

He took a step closer to her until only the two stair steps separated them. "But nothing. I'm really sorry, but whatever it is, you'll have to find someone else. The only pictures I'm taking on this trip are for me and me alone."

He watched her try to mask her desperation. The sun side-lit her features, creating shadows under her eyes. His fingers tensed. "I might make an exception if the favor includes you being the subject; otherwise the answer is no. Period."

April blanched. Taking pictures of her was the absolute last thing she'd ever ask him to do. "You're right. I shouldn't have asked." Embarrassed by both his apparent sincerity and the bungling mess she'd made of asking him for help, she stammered, "I . . . I'm sorry. I'll figure something out."

She paused, fighting for composure. She'd already practically begged the man—a paying guest—to help her out. He didn't need to be subjected to a list of her problems as well. "I'll let you get your rest, Mr. Tango. I'll have the desk call you at nine tomorrow morning, unless you wish otherwise."

"It's Jack. And nine sounds fine." She nodded, then turned to leave. Jack noticed a brown streak marring the sleeve of her blouse and reached out to brush at the stain, but dropped his hand immediately when she stiffened. His gaze darted to her face and found her quietly assessing him. "Your blouse. It's dirty. It must have been the strap of my gear bag."

She looked at her arm, obvious relief crossing her face when she spied the streak of dirt.

Something wasn't right here, he thought. Even though he'd mistaken the reason for her earlier persistence, her reaction just now didn't jibe. His annoyance fled. "Please put the cleaning tab for this on my bill."

"That won't be necessary."

"It'll make me feel better for being so rude to you."

"You weren't rude, just tired. If anyone was rude, it was me."

"Anyone ever tell you you're a lousy liar?"

She paused, looking away for a moment, then met his gaze directly. "Not when it counted, no," she responded evenly.

Again she surprised him. "Then they were blind." Her responding smile lit her features all the way up to her lovely brown eyes. Just standing there, being the recipient of it, seemed to infuse him with renewed strength. "Have breakfast with me tomorrow, after I've gotten some rest, and we'll talk. Okay?"

"Does that mean you'll consider my request?"

"You really are the CEO, aren't you?"

She lifted her shoulders slightly as if to say she had to try, but her smile was unapologetic. "Will you?"

"Only if you'll consider mine. I meant what I said about taking some pictures of you." Her smile became a memory. What had he said? "I was serious about being on vacation too. Any pictures I take while I'm here are for me and me alone. I don't intend to sell them, just appreciate them."

Seeing he hadn't eased her mind, he shrugged as if it didn't matter. He didn't want it to matter. "Forget I mentioned it, okay? But the breakfast offer still stands. I promise that with some sleep I won't embarrass you in public. Please?"

His "please" was accompanied by the crooked smile she'd already learned did dangerous things to her ability to reason. Sexy and so tempting. Too tempting. April argued with herself that it would be crazy to pass up a chance to change his mind. "I'd be glad to. Why don't we meet on the observation deck cafe. It's at the top of the main building facing the ocean."

"Sounds great. I always enjoy a beautiful view first thing in the morning."

"Fine. I'll see you then." April forced herself not to rush back down the path. And she absolutely refused to contemplate why his twinkling, green-eyed gaze had swept over her during his comment on his preference of morning scenery.

Or her immediate reaction to it.

❦━━━━━━━━━❦

April looked up from her morning tea to stare out over the deck railing, watching the morning waves roll relentlessly onto the beach. Each crest seemed like an endless second hand, ticking away the time on nature's eternal clock. Her time was running out.

She forced her gaze back to the tack sheets she'd picked up from Carmen's teenage nephew first thing that morning. "Smithson will flip," April muttered under her breath. She cringed at the blurry results of Alejandro's attempt at shooting yesterday's wedding rehearsal and dinner. "That is if the bride-to-be doesn't kill me first."

How on earth she was going to pull off a wedding of this caliber with a seventeen-year-old camera buff as her photographer? April's thoughts scattered as she felt the wispy hairs on the back of her neck stir in a way that had nothing to do with the windy morning. Jack Tango was around somewhere.

She barely managed to shove the sheets under her place mat before he took the seat across from her. She didn't stop to analyze just how she'd known it was him.

"Am I late?" His voice was raspy, as if he'd just awakened.

"No, not at all." Then she made the mistake of lifting her gaze to his face. Big mistake.

Gone was the shadow of a beard that had grazed his jaw. His dark blond hair was still a little wild, probably from the stiff morning breeze, but he hadn't been out in it long enough to dry more than the tips. He'd replaced the dusty cotton shirt with a yellow T-shirt that should have been rumpled, given his method of packing, but the breadth of his chest had stretched out any wrinkles.

None of those things were what made her wary, though they certainly accounted for her increased pulse rate. The guy cleaned up better than good, she thought, and purposely avoided wondering what he'd put on the lower half of his body. It was safer. If there was such a thing around him.

"Don't tell me. There's a dress code for break-fast, right?" The corner of his mouth curved in that little smile, making it clear he'd noticed her quick inventory. "I don't do tails before nine P.M., but I'll go back and put on a tie if it'll make you feel better."

April returned his smile, charmed despite herself with this new, improved, even sexier version of Jack Tango. Her sunny outlook clouded slightly as her gaze shifted from his dry smile to his eyes. Her first mistake had just become her second.

The rising sun at his back cast his face in shadows, making his eyes an almost incandescent green.

She'd convinced herself after leaving him in the bungalow yesterday that she'd overestimated their effect on her. As his gaze slowly took in her appearance, she knew she hadn't. Not in the least. "You look just fine," she assured him in complete honesty.

"May I return the compliment?"

He was just being polite, she told herself. His smile shouldn't have such a devastating effect. It was just a smile. But combined with those eyes . . .

Business, April. Concentrate on business. She shifted her gaze to the clipboard beside her plate. The long list of wedding details still left to be handled brought reality back with a thud. "Thank you, Mr. Tango."

"Just Jack," he quickly responded. A waiter appeared at his elbow, diverting his attention.

"*Buenos días, señor*," Jack greeted him. "*Huevos rancheros y una taza de café, por favor?*" The waiter nodded, then both men turned their attention to April, who stared back, openmouthed. "*Señora* Morgan?" Jack prodded.

"*Señorita*," April responded without thinking. Jack's smile snapped her back to attention and she quickly gave her order. "Thank you, Antonio," she said to the waiter. The older man nodded sharply and left.

"I said you could take me out in public."

April turned her attention back to Jack. "You

just ordered eggs and a cup of coffee like a native. Your Spanish is hardly accented, Mr.—" He arched one brow, and she relented. It would help for them to be friendly if she was going to get him to agree to her proposal. "Jack. If you speak the language so well, why all the trouble with Miguel yesterday?"

"I was kinda wiped out when I finally got here. I hadn't slept in . . ." Jack's voice trailed off and he began toying with his fork, looking away from her for the first time that morning. "Let's just say if I hadn't gotten horizontal quickly, my body would have made the decision for me. Your bellman spoke some kind of local mix and I guess I wasn't being too accommodating." He lifted his gaze back to hers. "Did I get him in trouble?"

"No, of course not. Miguel has worked for me for a long time, almost since we started. He places a lot of importance on his job. He takes pride in it, but he can be a bit . . ."

"Overeager?" The corner of his mouth curved again.

"Just a little. He was only trying to do his job, but I apologize if he bothered you." She paused, then took a small breath before continuing. "Everything is okay, though? Your bags, I mean. Nothing damaged?"

"Are you asking me as the resort owner making sure her guest is happy, or as the lady who needs a certain equipment in one piece for some personal reason?"

April had the good grace to flush. She hadn't thought she'd been so obvious. Matching wits with a fatigued Jack Tango yesterday had been challenging enough. She began to wonder if anything got by those piercing eyes that missed nothing—and noticed everything.

She thought of the blurry tack sheets under her place mat. The wedding ceremony was to take place in less than ten hours. She had nothing left to lose. April took a sip of her tea and carefully replaced the cup before chancing a direct look. "Both."

Jack's neutral expression eased back into a grin as he nodded. "Bravo, *señorita*. With me, honesty will get you where flattery never will. But my answer stays the same."

"Aren't you the least bit curious why I'd ask a favor of a guest?" April watched him closely, but the only outward response she could interpret as interest were the dilating pupils of his eyes. "Would you at least hear me out?"

"I didn't remain conscious for too long after you left my bungalow yesterday, but what lucid time I had left was spent wondering how a slight thing like you managed a resort this size." He paused for a long moment. "I think you just gave me my answer. You wear the opposition down."

April struggled to keep her smile in place.

Was that his version of a "yes"? Oh well, she thought, bracing herself. No guts, no photographer. "I couldn't help but notice your equipment yesterday."

"Yes, I noticed that, too."

Her confidence faltered as her strategy took a direct hit. A grin that was far from polite creased his handsome face. She fought the flame creeping into her cheeks at his obvious interpretation and bulled ahead. "You are a professional?"

"One of the best." His grin widened, exposing two even rows of gleaming white teeth that only a fool wouldn't consider predatory.

Well, April thought, she may have been a fool once, but never again. It had been the sort of lesson she wasn't likely to forget. And running this resort wasn't a picnic either. She could certainly handle one sexy, rough-around-the-edges photographer. "You do get paid for taking pictures, don't you?" she reiterated evenly.

"Have you reconsidered my offer then?" he countered, neatly sidestepping the issue again. "If you're worried about my fees, don't. The photos I take of you will fall under the heading of pleasure, not business."

His confidence where she was concerned irked her even further. "I'm afraid that just isn't possible," she stated politely, then quickly backpedaled as his smile faded again. The Cove needed his help and she couldn't risk the fiasco that was certain to occur if she failed to get him to agree. Just because he'd apparently taken on a personal agenda in the matter was no reason to give up.

Even if the agenda's only item seemed to be her.

"I'm certain you'll be able to find someone here at the resort who'll be more than willing to—"

"I didn't ask someone else, I asked you." He spoke softly, but the underlying element of steel made it clear he'd been insulted. "Not because you were the first woman I ran into when I arrived. Not because you run the resort. And not for some kind of damn trade." He stopped abruptly, then averted his gaze. He picked up his fork, trying to balance the long handle on his finger. He studied the seesawing piece of silver as if it would somehow divine an answer to whatever he was privately debating.

Before she could comment, he pinned her with his gaze.

"I've changed my mind about that last part."

April tried to ignore the intensity he injected into such a simple phrase and focus on its meaning. "In what way?"

"It's very simple. I'll do whatever you want, within reason, if you'll pose for me."

"You don't even know what I want!" She didn't try to hide her surprise at his sudden turnaround.

"You're right, I don't. But I can't imagine the

CEO of a major resort asking a guest to do something illegal. And it can't be kinky, since you turn ten shades of crimson at even the slightest innuendo of anything sexual." He flashed a quick grin when she did it again. "So, do we have a deal?"

April's mouth had dropped open after his first sentence and it took a moment before she was able to snap it shut. She worked hard on making her mouth curve into her best resort-owner smile. "You're right, it's nothing illegal," she said in a voice that was still a shade too strained to be nonchalant. Refusing to even comment on the rest of his statement, she went on. "It won't take more than a couple of hours away from your vacation. Which, by the way, I'm fully prepared to pick up the tab for in return for your help."

"As I said before, I don't want your money."

Her eyes narrowed. "What, exactly, do you want?" Her voice was even, betraying none of the emotions roiling inside.

"One hour of your time for every one I give to you."

Her disappointment was swift and surprisingly deep. Her fault, she thought. She shouldn't have expected him to be different. He'd learn, as others had, that she didn't barter herself for business.

Then again, April sensed that if she pushed much further on the issue of her reluctance to be photographed, she'd have an entirely new problem to deal with. For whatever reason, she'd managed to intrigue Jack Tango. And the very last thing she needed was for someone with camera equipment and an incredible power of observation to focus either of those things on her private life. She couldn't risk the Cove's reputation on the chance that he wouldn't find anything out.

Besides, she thought, he'd said one hour of her time for every one of his. He hadn't specified she had to spend hers posing. "It's a deal. On one condition." Jack looked honestly surprised at her answer. Good. She enjoyed having the upper hand for a change.

"Which is?"

"That I give my return hours as it suits my schedule. I'm going to need your help this evening, but I'm afraid I won't have much, if any, free time over the next few days."

Jack nodded, then looked up as the waiter approached with their meals. "Since I'm going to be here for a couple of weeks, I imagine we'll have plenty of time to work out your . . . payment."

Several minutes passed while Jack ate his eggs and April tried to digest his interpretation of "payment." Jack had more success with his meal.

"Are you going to eat the rest of your toast, or turn it into more bird feed?"

April looked down at her plate to find one half of her slice of toast shredded into little bits. She'd managed to take a whole bite out of the other half. Pushing her plate away, she picked up her tea and took a sip, wondering why she was always the one searching for control when they were together.

"If you're done with that, may I?" He gestured to her plate. "I missed a few meals along with the sleep."

"Help yourself. I can call the waiter so you can—" She broke off as he picked up her slice of toast and turned it, sinking his teeth into the same spot she had.

His gaze met hers over the crusty edge as he took another bite. She sat there, transfixed as he polished off the crispy slice, one tantalizing bite at a time. She'd deny it to anyone who asked, but Jack Tango turned the simple act of eating toast into an erotic event. If he licked the butter off his fingers, she swore she'd dump the entire pot of tea in his lap.

"No need for a waiter," he said finally, thankfully using the linen napkin to wipe his hands. "I'll admit to having a big appetite, but sometimes it just takes something small and tasty to satisfy it."

While she was busy trying to decide if there was a hidden meaning in that statement, he dropped the real bomb.

"As for our deal, I don't care when you put in your time. But I do mean to collect, *mi cielo*. And my services don't come cheap."

April stared hard at Jack, her defenses instantly back on full alert. Somehow, in the space of a day, Jack Tango had breached walls she'd spent ten years building. Maybe she'd been a fool all along and just hadn't been tested.

More probably it was his unwitting use of the Spanish endearment she'd thought never to hear again.

Mi cielo. My sky.

She ignored the swift pain of unforgotten memories. There was no way he could have known how much hearing those words would hurt. Just the same, the memory served to insure that whatever it was about him that triggered such a strong attraction would have to stop. Right here. Right now. No amount of spontaneous physical combustion was worth that kind of risk.

"I'm certain we can come to an agreement." She placed her napkin on her empty place mat. "I'm sorry, but I have to go. I know you must be starving, so please let me send Antonio back over. Our menu is a bit eclectic, but I'm sure you'll find something you'll like. Our chef is French, but he prides himself on his adaptability." Her nerves were making her ramble. She stopped, quickly gathered her clipboard and cellular phone, and stood.

"Pride is a big thing around here." His voice was steady, with no discernible inflection to reveal his mood.

She risked one last look at him. "I think that's one concept we both understand."

"And I think we understand a whole lot more than that."

April took a second too long to react and he reached for her wrist before she could move away. She stilled, looked down at her wrist imprisoned in his gentle, but firm grip, then stared directly at him. "Let go of me, please."

He immediately complied. "I'm sorry, no offense intended." His tone was sincere. "I just wondered if, before you ran off, you'd like to end the suspense and tell me what it is I just agreed to do?"

April's face heated. She felt like an overly sensitive idiot. "Of course."

Jack leaned across the table and slid the forgotten tack sheets out from under her place mat. "Would it have anything to do with these?"

She nodded mutely, but Jack didn't notice. He was already flipping through them.

"Terrible. A complete waste of good film," he muttered.

"You make taking poor pictures sound like a crime. I know they're bad, but—"

"Unless these are pictures of the Headless Horseman at a family reunion, they're the worst things I've ever seen." He looked up at her, disgust showing plainly on his face. "Please, tell me you didn't shoot these."

April couldn't help it. Her lips twitched into a dry smile. "Why? Do you have some criteria about only working for someone who can handle a camera as well as you? Wouldn't that make you a bit dispensable?"

Given his track record, she'd fully expected a sarcastic response. Instead he looked as if his entire body had just been interred in a deep freeze. His shoulders tensed and his fingers gripped the glossy photos for a never-ending second before they slowly flexed, allowing the sheets to drop back onto the table. She watched the rigid line of his back slowly relax and the tendons in his neck smooth. Apparently she'd hit a major nerve. Well, turnabout was fair play, she thought, although she gained no satisfaction from it.

"I'm sorry. Really. I was kidding."

"I know you were." He sighed, then tilted his head back to look up at her, a shadow of his usually dry smile curving his lips. "It's just ironic that the reason I'm here is to prove exactly that."

"Exactly what?"

"That I'm dispensable."

THREE

"You may kiss the bride."

Jack waited as the groom lifted the bride's veil. He released the shutter just as the young man gazed into the eyes of his wife for the first time, capturing for eternity the private look of love and trust that passed between them in that special moment.

When the newlyweds continued kissing, cheers and a smattering of applause broke out from the guests.

Irritated for some reason, Jack wondered if the couple planned on breathing sometime in the near future, or if they were just giving a new meaning to the vow "till death do us part." He ran off a few shots, then quickly moved to get several more of the young couple as they walked down the narrow white rug that had been rolled across the east lawn in honor of the occasion.

He packed his equipment and headed for the large mass of floral arrangements that served as an altar. "Jack Tango shooting a wedding," he grumbled, thinking that being dispensable might not always be a bad thing. Thank God Franklin hadn't witnessed this. After years in friendly competition, Franklin would give his right lung to see his Pulitzer prize-winning colleague and close friend reduced to using his talents for assembling a debutante's wedding album. Jack had never been one to flaunt his achievements, but anyone familiar with his work would have to agree this was a bit like asking Paul Prudhomme to put together a few peanut butter and jelly sandwiches. Overkill.

He pasted a smile on his face and yanked up his damned cummerbund again. The absent Steve had apparently taken advantage of the daily buffets during his tenure as staff photographer. As Jack adjusted the tripod, his gaze scanned the crowd, instantly zeroing in on April with an unerring accuracy he'd given up trying to figure out hours ago. He watched as she smiled and skillfully moved from one cluster of reception guests to the next, leaving smiles in her wake. The lady knew how to work a room. Her guests were content.

It came as a bit of a shock, but for all his grousing, so was he. He'd convinced himself he'd only jumped on the crazy trade idea as a way to get the attractive CEO to spend some time alone with him. Although he had to admit it was a rather unique predicament for him.

He watched her smile fade a bit as she lifted her one and only glass of champagne and surreptitiously surveyed the crowd, and admitted to himself that his physical response to her was only a small part of it. Even with her diminutive stature, she had this incredibly dynamic presence, not surprising considering she ran such a successful resort. Yet there was an underlying sense of something being wrong. Something very much like fear. But fear of what? His journalistic instincts hinted that she must be hiding something. Or from something.

Earlier at breakfast, he'd sidestepped her questions about his cryptic statement regarding his dispensability by getting her to explain her reasons for needing his help. As she'd explained the details, she'd seemed very concerned. Too concerned for what had to be just another typical problem in an operation this size.

He watched as April lowered her glass without tasting the expensive wine, her gaze raking over the crowd again. He started to follow her gaze, automatically trying to determine what she was looking for, then abruptly stopped. "No, I am *not* getting involved here." Cursing Franklin for sending him here in the first place, he turned back to the group assembling before him and forced his mind to the task at hand.

Grimacing, hoping it passed for a smile, he ran off two shots of the grandmother's brothers on the bride's side, then paused while someone went off in search of the groom's great-uncles or whatever. He turned to check on his film supply, praying it was near an end, and caught a brief glimpse of April as she crossed the lawn to shake hands with the bride and groom. She smiled, then laughed at something the groom whispered in her ear.

Without thinking, he raised the camera hanging around his neck and ran off a few shots. Her face, flushed with laughter and happiness for the newlyweds, was a surprising revelation. It occurred to him that, while she'd always been polite, and had even smiled at him, he'd never once seen her look so . . . carefree.

What had happened to make a woman so obviously warm and sharing by nature suppress those traits and hold herself apart? He'd known her less than twenty-four hours and he'd already seen all the signs. He was intimately familiar with them. They were the same ones that stared back at him every time he looked in the mirror.

"Excuse me, young man, but could you please get a picture of us? I'm certain Deborah would want it for her album."

"Huh?" was Jack's less than professional reply.

He jerked around to find a group of elderly women, all clad in what could only be described as wedding muumuus, smiling up at him. "Why certainly, ladies."

Jack smiled in relief at the diversion, instinctively switching on the easy charm he'd long ago developed as a tool to maintain the crucial mental distance between photojournalist and subject. Smile and the world smiled with you, that was his motto. "The wedding album wouldn't be complete without a shot of such a lovely group."

An hour later, Jack was swearing quietly and quite fluently in several languages, all pretense of patience close to being gone as he waited for someone to track down dear old Aunt Minnie for what would absolutely be the final photo—at least if he had anything to say about it.

Never, ever again would he let some pushy, raven-haired sprite, with eyes that held way too many secrets, con him into doing something like this. Never mind that the trade was his idea. No payoff was worth this sort of pain-in-the-butt work.

As he waited for the group in front of him to get organized, he found himself scanning the crowds again. It was then that he noticed April on the receiving end of a hug from Senator Smithson. And hating it, given her pale, tight-lipped expression. All of his journalistic instincts should have gone on red alert, but they were detoured around a sudden intense rush of . . .

What, Tango? Protectiveness? Jealousy? Come on, he argued with himself, the man's old enough to be April's father. Or a friend of her father's. Jack's professional instincts rebounded into instant sharp focus.

He motioned to Alejandro, who'd come to help after his shift in the dining room ended. Honestly not caring whether Aunt Minnie's head made it into the photo or not, Jack quickly went over what to push and where to aim, then grabbed a more powerful zoom lens and exchanged lenses on the camera around his neck.

Jack quickly skirted the small crowd, careful not to jostle any elbows or trays of drinks in his efforts to get a clear view of April and the good Senator before they finished their conversation.

Senator Smithson was holding her at arm's length now, as if admiring either April or her dress. Jack had already given his seal of approval to the stunning fuchsia dress. The halter-style top showcased the graceful curve from neck to shoulder, and the full skirt swished just the right amount to make him harden up whenever he caught her walking away from him. He made a quick mental note to pull the shots he'd taken of her this afternoon before giving the proofs to the bride.

Jack moved in behind the long tables that had

been set up to hold the assortment of finger food and the elaborate wedding cake. He trained the lens on April's face, zoomed in, and brought it into focus. Senator Smithson blocked his view for a second. When he drew back, Jack went completely still—still in the way only someone who'd tiptoed through war zones could do so completely. His instincts hadn't failed him. Her skin was as bright as her dress.

Jack responded instantly. He quickly started around the tables. Never taking his eyes off her, he swore silently at the seemingly endless array of food.

Smiling, Smithson made another remark, apparently unaware of the effect his words had on her. Then Jack saw her sway as if her knees had buckled. That did it. With one hand planted firmly between the tray of quesadillas and the French tortes, Jack vaulted over the table in a graceful leap.

April felt a callused hand grip her elbow and turned to find Jack smiling at her. He'd materialized out of nowhere. Before she could say anything, he pulled her closer and put a supporting arm gently around her waist, clamping his hand on her hip and extending his right one to Senator Smithson.

"Lovely wedding, Senator. You must be proud." Jack pumped the man's hand exuberantly and anchored her hip more firmly against his thigh.

Looking nonplussed, the silver-haired gentleman slowly recovered. "Yes, Deb is my only daugh-

ter. Don't believe I caught your name, young man."
His gravelly Texas drawl was as thick as the lenses
of his glasses.

Jack watched closely as the distinguished politician squinted his magnified eyes, damning himself
for not thinking clearly enough to realize the Senator might recognize him. His assignments were
usually international and rarely involved U.S. poli-
tics, but with modern technology the world could
be a rather small community.

"Aren't you—"

"The resort photographer? Why, yes. Ms. Morgan hired me personally just to do this wedding."
He dropped Smithson's hand and lifted the camera
dangling from his chest as if to prove his statement.

"Yes, well, I'm sure you're doing a fine job."

Jack breathed a small sigh of relief as the Senator's expression once again became that of a proud
father.

"I confess I just bankrolled the shindig," he
went on. "Martha—that's the wife—she handled
all the details."

April was still leaning on him, a surprisingly overt show of need for her and one he'd bet
his prize Hasselblad she'd regret later. But it was
enough to decide him on his course of action.

April was confused by Jack's behavior, but she
was too busy praying the old man would just go

away to worry about it. Another minute and she'd pass out just from the stress of keeping a smile on her face. Jack suddenly loosened his grip and she shifted more heavily against him.

"That's right, lean on me, *mi cielo*," Jack whispered in her ear as the Senator droned on about his daughter. "Trust me."

She stiffened and tried to pull away. "Thanks, but I can han—" Her whispered response was cut off as Jack tightened his hold and shifted his attention back to Smithson.

"You know, Senator. I don't believe I got a shot of you and your lovely wife. Martha, is it?" Jack linked his arm through the unwitting politician's gesturing one, and deftly steered both the older gentleman and April back to the refreshment table before either could protest.

"As a matter of fact, I think—"

"Now, let me get Ms. Morgan here a plate," Jack interrupted the politician smoothly. "I'm sure you know all about workaholics, Senator. Never make the time to eat. If it wasn't for her staff, Ms. Morgan would just waste away."

Jack kept up the nonstop stream of bull and April was too caught off guard to stop him. Besides, after the bomb the Senator had just unwittingly dropped on her, she gladly accepted Jack's unspoken offer to run interference for a few minutes. Before she knew it, she was seated in a folding lawn chair with a plate of food in one hand and a cup of punch in the other. By the time she balanced everything and looked up to thank Jack for coming to her rescue, he was halfway across the lawn, still towing the Senator in his wake.

April absentmindedly bit into the cheese-filled tortilla as she watched Jack corral an elegant platinum blonde she recognized as Martha Smithson and proceed to charm her as well. Just how he had known the precise moment April needed him she didn't know. But she wasn't foolish enough to think his help came without a price.

Several times during the ceremony, as well as during the reception, she'd turned to find his intense gaze focused on her. She'd stopped questioning how she always knew it was him. The idea that she was just as intrigued by him as he apparently was with her was just too unsettling to even contemplate.

She forced her gaze away from his tall, lean figure and back to her plate. It didn't help. She couldn't erase the gorgeous picture that was Jack Tango in black tie and tails. So what if the jacket pulled too tightly at his shoulders and the back seam looked as if it would split each time he leaned over to line up a shot? So what if his cummerbund kept slipping down his lean hips, constantly drawing her eyes to the fit of his pleated pants? All men looked good in tuxes.

It was the fact that she kept picturing Jack Tango out of his that disturbed her.

And he'd called her *mi cielo* again. The last time she'd heard that endearment, before meeting Jack, was permanently seared in her brain. Her father had used his pet name for her almost mercilessly while trying to persuade his daughter not to file sexual harassment charges against her boss, Alan Markham. Markham also happened to be an investment partner of her father's, not to mention a newly announced candidate for the state senate.

He'd stopped using any pet names long before her case came to trial. Then his reputation had been dragged through the mud right along with hers. The names he'd used after that were far from endearing. Now he didn't call her anything at all.

And now, ten years later, she had to come to grips with the fact that Alan Markham, the man she'd unsuccessfully tried to keep out of the senate, the same man who had pulled out all the stops to humiliate and degrade her in front of an entire nation, was about to announce his candidacy for president of the United States.

Her food lodged in her suddenly constricted throat. She had to get out of here. Placing her half-eaten quesadilla back on her plate, she handed both that and her cup to a passing waiter. Rising, she motioned to Carmen. After making sure everything was under control, she quickly found the newlyweds and said her good-byes, though she doubted they'd even remember later. They'd barely unglued their eyes from one another since the bride had taken her first step down the aisle.

Ignoring the rush of melancholy that accompanied that thought, she scanned the crowd for the Senator and his wife. It would be less than polite to leave without saying good-bye and personally checking to make sure they weren't in need of anything else, but she wanted desperately to avoid any further contact. She finally spied them about ten yards away.

They seemed preoccupied. Not surprising; Jack was still with them. She ducked her head before he could turn and find her staring at him and quickly left by the side lawn. Her mind was still reeling, and more than anything she needed to get away from everything and everyone to clear her head. Not stopping to wonder who she was avoiding more, the Senator or Jack, she ducked into the cool hallway and hurried toward her office.

Jack looked up from his conversation with Mrs. Smithson just in time to see April duck into a side door. *Damn.* He wanted to go after her. Instead he forced himself to take another sip of ice-cold water. He'd have plenty of time to find out what had happened between the Senator and April. He glanced at his watch. Five hours' worth, according to his calculations.

He just hoped she didn't plan on pulling any stunts to get out of fulfilling her part of the bargain. Because, whether she knew it or not, they had just passed the game-playing stage of their relationship.

In the meantime, he planned to make the most of his conversation with the Senator.

April turned up the path to bungalow 14, the desire to run in the opposite direction growing stronger with every step she took. She went over again what she planned to say to Jack. She hadn't seen him, not even a glimpse, since she'd fled from the ceremony two days ago. She'd told herself she was relieved. She hadn't been kidding about having a packed schedule.

Most of the wedding party was still residing at the resort, all except for the Senator and his wife, who'd left just after the newlyweds yesterday morning. She'd thought she might see Jack at the festive send-off at the resort heliport. But there'd been no sign of him that morning. Or for the twenty-four hours that had followed.

As far as she could tell, without questioning anyone too closely, he'd made no effort to contact her at all.

Until two hours ago, when her concierge, Dom, had casually informed her that Señor Jack had left word at the desk that he'd like to see her at her earliest possible convenience. She'd put off coming by, convincing herself the front desk needed her help in checking in a mad rush of conference attendees. But her staff was well trained and she quickly ran out of things to do. She couldn't put off her meeting with Jack any longer. And now that the time had come, she actually felt a certain sense of relief.

She blew at an errant strand of hair the morning wind had dislodged from her French twist and stepped up onto the porch. Funny how isolated the bungalow suddenly seemed. She usually loved the scent of the bougainvillea which draped the stuccoed porch railings of the private bungalows. Now it seemed cloying and inhibitive.

Forcing an uneven breath in and out of her lungs, she raised her hand to rap on the door, silently praying that she could get Jack to agree to her terms of payment.

The door eased open at her light knock. She waited for a moment, bracing herself for the instant that she'd face him again. After several seconds that seemed like hours, she realized no one was coming. She leaned in to pull the door shut, surprised he'd leave his door unlocked with all his expensive and cherished equipment inside, and heard the unmistakable sounds of a shower running. Her hand froze in mid-reach as images of Jack, naked in the shower, flashed through her mind in picture-perfect clarity.

Shaking off the provocative visions of water cascading over his tall, muscular form, she rapidly debated the merits of retreat. But while her mind was busy making a case for going back to work, her body decided to go on in and make itself at home. She pushed the door closed behind her, then changed her mind and left it open an inch or two, hoping that the knowledge of that small margin of escape would give her the strength to see this through without faltering.

She wandered over to the small couch. The duffel bag was gone, but he'd wasted no time making himself at home. She ran a finger over the yellow T-shirt carelessly tossed over the back of the couch, then around the rim of an empty bottle of beer sitting on the rattan end table. Upon encountering a damp spot on the rim, she snatched her finger away, suddenly realizing the inherent intimacy of her actions.

She was debating whether or not to call out and announce her presence, when her attention was caught by the open zipper pockets of the small bag she'd carried into this room several days ago. It wasn't the bag specifically, but the glossy photos that poked out of one of the side pockets that she'd noticed. Telling herself they were probably wedding photos, and that as Jack's employer for that event she had every right to see them, she slid the glossy prints carefully out of the bag.

They were upside down, so she turned them around—and found her own eyes staring back at her. Confused, since she was the sole subject of the picture, she quickly sifted through the rest of the dozen or so shots. She was the focus of all of them.

Embarrassment over being caught unawares was quickly usurped by indignation over his tactics. *How dare he!* Forcing the red haze from her vision, she went through the stack again, painfully scrutinizing each one, as if trying to emblazon the proof of his duplicity forever in her brain. Like she'd actually forget!

In one shot, he'd caught her staring off at some distant point, as if deep in thought. There was one of her laughing with the bride and groom. She immediately tucked that one under the stack, ignoring the glowing expression he'd captured forever on film. She stared long and hard at the next one and her hand trembled a bit. She looked so . . . alone. A heavy weight settled somewhere deep inside her chest as she realized he'd snapped this one the split second before the newlyweds had kissed for the first time.

Her anger fled, replaced by a pressure squeezing around her heart, the tightness a result of having to confront her inner self, over and over. Each shot revealed, in brilliant color, all of the emotions she'd long ago buried in an effort to heal her soul. Her entire body stiffened as she flipped to the next-to-last photo.

She knew instantly that she'd been looking directly at Jack when he'd taken this one. Her slightly parted lips, the flush on her cheeks, the intense awareness in her eyes . . .

April suddenly slapped the photos back together, almost crumpling them as she shoved them back into the side pocket in her haste to erase the image of how she'd looked at Jack. With hunger. A deep, unabiding hunger.

Blushing hotly, she whirled away from the bag, only to be confronted with the translucent gaze of Jack's green eyes.

Leaning against the bedroom doorway, a white towel wrapped around his hips and beads of water still scattered through the swirl of dark hair on his chest, he assessed her silently. She couldn't have said how long she stood there, absorbing his gaze as it slowly traveled over every inch of her, but it felt like somewhere between a heartbeat and a lifetime.

"Do you like them?" Other than his mouth, he didn't move even the tiniest muscle.

Arms crossed around her midsection, neither did she. "Did you honestly think I would? Is that why you took them?"

"I told you before that anything other than wedding pictures would be for me and me alone. But, yes, I guess I had hoped you'd like them."

"I thought I'd made it more than clear that I didn't want to be the subject of any photographs."

"And I thought we had a deal."

Up till now his voice had been soft and quiet, but neutral, as if her answers weren't all that important. But his last statement revealed the tight control he was fighting to maintain, and April took an unconscious step backward.

"The deal was one hour of my time for one of yours. You said nothing about posing for you."

Jack shifted his weight off of the door frame, but didn't step into the room. "Back to playing word games? Just what sort of payment did you have in mind, April? Is that why you're here?"

His gaze traveled slowly over her face, scrutinizing each feature, the sheer intensity of it like a flame caressing her body. His expression was unreadable except for the brilliant incandescence of his eyes, and she couldn't tell if that was from anger . . . or desire.

Suddenly aware of the change in her situation and desperately wanting to escape, April eyed the sunlit sliver of freedom behind her.

"Leave, if that's what you truly want. I won't stop you. But you're only postponing this conversation."

Despite his assurance, she felt trapped, and hated it every bit as much now as she had years ago when Markham had cornered her in his office. She broke off that train of thought and said, "As far as I'm concerned those pictures constitute payment in full. End of conversation." She whirled to leave but a strong hand imprisoned her wrist with lightning speed. She'd never heard him leave the doorway.

"Not so fast, *Señorita* Morgan." Jack gentled his grip immediately when she stopped her flight. He tugged slowly until she turned to face him and waited patiently for her to look directly at him. When she did, he silently cheered her for having the nerve to do so, then cursed himself for being the reason he read fear in those lovely golden-brown eyes.

"If you want my attention in the future, just ask." Her voice was low and even.

"If you wouldn't run away every time the conversation gets tricky I wouldn't have to resort to this."

"Let me go." She enunciated each word slowly.

"If I promise not to touch you, will you stay and talk this thing out? Please?"

She nodded once and he immediately dropped her wrist. "Always remember you can trust me, April. But never forget I place a high priority on keeping one's word."

Her eyes widened in shock and anger, making him want to smile at the return of the April Morgan whose spirit had so enthralled him. The seriousness of the conversation made him refrain. "I never said I wouldn't take pictures of you." His voice softened slightly. "But I did say they would remain personal. If you knew me better, you'd know that my word is one of my most valued possessions."

He paused for a moment, watching her chin remain firm as her lips drew into a flat line. The edge left his voice completely as he asked the question he most wanted an answer to. "Do you really mind so much that I want them?"

He felt rather than saw the fight go out of her. The defeat in her soft brown eyes touched a place so deep inside him he'd long ago forgotten its hiding place. Why now? he questioned silently, after years of scrupulously maintaining a careful distance, avoiding anything that even hinted at getting emotionally involved. Why her?

But there were no quick, easy answers. He looked into eyes that moments ago had flashed with a vibrancy that captivated him. Now they had dulled in defeat, and he felt a fist of need tighten inside him. A need to make her smile again, to find what was wrong in her world and right it, a need so intense it should have sent him running in the other direction.

Instead he moved closer. More than anything, he wanted to touch her, comfort her. But he'd promised not to. He settled for lifting his finger until it was a hairbreadth away from her lips. Their gazes locked, then his shifted lower as he traced an imaginary line over her bottom lip.

He curled his finger into his palm and let his hand drop. "No one will ever see them but me. I swear it." Her lips parted, but she said nothing. He blew out a deep breath, his promise warring with his need to kiss the life back into her.

But he wanted an equal participant when they kissed for the first time. They both deserved nothing less. "Can I trust you to stay here for a few moments while I change?" Her reaction was as swift and sharp as he'd hoped it would be, but he wished he could have kissed her instead.

She took two steps away from him, brown eyes narrowed in anger. "If you knew me, you wouldn't have had to ask," she retorted, tossing his words back at him.

Without a word he turned and left the room. He closed the bedroom door and rested against it. The tempest was still present. Whatever he'd said or done to cause her to momentarily cave in hadn't completely doused the flame burning between them.

Jack let out a soft, self-deprecating laugh as he crossed the small room. He was here to rest, to give his body and soul some downtime and to decompress a little. So what did he do? He went right off and did what he'd managed to avoid in his entire thirty-five years on the planet. He'd gotten involved.

"Bad timing, Tango," he muttered. But he knew he had no choice. Like it or not, April Morgan had his complete and total attention.

Jack loosened the knot in the towel, letting it drop in a heap on the tiled floor. His smile returned as he grudgingly accepted the inevitability of his involvement. April didn't know it yet, but she'd just gained a formidable ally.

And a very determined future lover.

FOUR

April waited the space of a single heartbeat after hearing the click of the bedroom door before backing up a step and sinking down onto the small sofa.

Just who in the hell is Jack Tango anyway? she wondered, trying and failing to come up with an easy answer. He infuriated her with his blunt, overconfident remarks, mystified her by reacting to her cool comebacks with an approving glint in his eye . . . and scared the living hell out of her by reducing to ashes, with no more than a hint of a smile and a few softly spoken words, her firm decision to remain untouched by him.

She tried to gather her wits and form them back into her earlier resolve, but her gaze kept skipping back to the bedroom door, her mind to the man behind it. She never once looked at the door to freedom.

She saw the doorknob twist and experienced a similar feeling in her stomach. Jack stepped into the small living room, his face concealed by the white towel that he was using to dry his hair with. He stopped after a step or two and slung the towel in the general direction of the low wooden table in the breakfast nook that, along with a tiny kitchen, formed the other half of the bungalow.

He was wearing a rumpled cotton shirt in a wild native print and faded red shorts just brief enough to keep her staring at the tanned, slightly hairy expanse of muscular thighs and calves underneath the tattered edges.

"Thanks," he said.

She yanked her gaze up to his, expecting to find a smug smile plastered on his sexy face at being caught gawking at his legs. Instead his expression was carefully neutral. "For what?"

"For being here. For wanting to stay and work this out." He turned toward the kitchen, calling over his shoulder, "I meant to restock the fridge yesterday; all I have is beer. Want one?"

"No. Thanks. I still have work to do this after—" She gulped as her gaze moved automatically from watching his backside to observing the bunching of his bicep as he twisted off the cap of his beer.

"—noon," she finished weakly. This was insanity. And it had just gotten worse; this time he'd caught her looking.

She averted her gaze and cleared her throat to speak, but Jack cut in before she could begin. It was just as well. She didn't have a clue as to what she was going to say anyway.

He perched on the arm of the couch at the opposite end from her. "Don't you ever take some time off?" He tilted the bottle up and swallowed a long draft before looking back at her.

She knew she was in trouble when she didn't respond until she'd finished watching his throat muscles contract as he swallowed. Was there anything this man couldn't turn into a sensual experience? "I . . . I don't have a regularly scheduled day off, if that's what you mean. But don't worry, I had every intention of keeping up my end of the agreement"

He held a hand up to stop her, then wiped his damp palm on his shorts, unintentionally drawing her gaze back to his thigh. April didn't care if he'd think she was incredibly rude, but she shifted her position and stared out of the window. It had to be safer.

"I didn't ask because of our stupid agreement. Call it professional curiosity. I just wondered what you do when all this"—he made a sweeping gesture with his arm—"gets to be too much. Even in a place this beautiful and peaceful, the pressure of running a business this size must get to you."

"Sometimes. But I'm used to it. It's what I do."

"Why?" She stiffened and he added, "I meant, why did you decide to build a resort out in the middle of nowhere?"

She relaxed and smiled, choosing to remember the better reasons. "My grandfather had land here. I spent a few summers with him. He ran a small charter-fishing business. That business eventually became Paradise Cove."

"How long ago did he die?"

The question startled her, making her instantly aware of how far she'd let her guard drop. At some point during her explanation she'd turned to face him again. The way he looked at her . . . She had this insane impulse just to blurt out the whole story to him, but she immediately stifled it. She'd be a fool to trust those probing eyes of his so easily. "Eight years." In response to his raised eyebrow, she added, "No, it wasn't easy, but I had a lot of help here. There are a few people still on staff who were quite loyal to my grandfather."

Eager to change the subject before he asked any more questions, she said, "Earlier, you used the phrase 'professional curiosity.' Why? Does your profession keep you from relaxing?"

"I've been accused of overdoing it a bit," he said dryly. "Actually, that's why I'm here. A friend of mine managed to convince me that a small break wouldn't kill me." He chuckled softly. "Although after twenty-seven rolls of Aunt Minnie and Uncle Jeets and the rest of the illustrious Smithsons, I'm not too sure it won't kill *him*."

April turned back to face him. The laughter in his light words had failed to cover the underlying fatigue, and if she wasn't mistaken, a trace of unrest. "Is that part of what you meant the other day? About being dispensable, I mean? Are you afraid of being fired?"

This time his laugh was more natural. "No. That's the least of my worries. I guess it's just that my career always seemed like one big vacation to me anyway and . . ." He trailed off for a moment, and this time he was the one to look out the front window. "I don't know, somewhere along the way it stopped being fun and started being a job."

"What exactly do you do?"

"I really don't want to talk about it." His casual shrug took any harshness out of his words. "For the time being I'm more interested in learning how to relax."

Even lounging on the arm of the couch, barefooted and with a beer in one hand, an aura of tension radiated around him. April felt the heat of embarrassment crawl up her neck. "Mr. Tango—" His head whipped around, his expression almost fierce. "Jack," she corrected quickly. He calmed a bit and so did April. Calling him by his last name had seemed strange and formal to her, too. "I've done nothing but bitch and moan since I walked in here. I'm sorry. I never got the chance to tell you how grateful the Cove is for—"

"I didn't do it for Paradise Cove, *mi cielo*." If Jack had hoped to make her feel better with his heartfelt statement, he'd failed miserably. Her entire body went stiff as a tree and her golden skin paled considerably. He immediately shifted to sit beside her. "April?" When she didn't turn he started to reach out, then pulled back. "Will you look at me?"

She turned to face him, a measure of respect reflected in her eyes, making him glad he'd kept his word. "What did I say? Does the idea that someone would want to help you frighten you?"

April read only true concern in his eyes. She saw no trace of ulterior motives. She ignored the tiny voice that whispered it probably wouldn't make a difference if she did. She wanted to confide in him. She needed to.

"I'm sorry. It's not your fault really, you couldn't have known."

"What's not my fault? This is the second time I've seen you freeze up like that after I've said something. Tell me what it is that bothers you."

"It's silly really. It's just that . . ." She let a small

sigh escape, steeling herself to face the memories that would surely come with the explanation.

"What, April? I can't prevent it from happening again if you don't tell me." He curled his fingers into his palm to keep from stroking her face. "You can trust me."

She pulled back just slightly and he shifted away a few inches, sensing this was difficult for her.

"My, uh . . . my father used to call me that."

"Call you what?" Confused, Jack broke off, going over what he'd said to her just now. She could only mean one thing. "You mean *mi cielo*? But that's a fairly common Mexican endearment, why should it bother you?" He saw her slump a little, as if someone had released a knot in her spine. "I'm sorry. Has he passed away?"

"No, he's very much alive. And yes, it was a term of affection he used with me. But that was a long time ago."

Her tone softened, as if she were very far away. The sense of loss, of grief, was so real he'd been sure her father had died. There was a world of hurt in her voice and in her posture, and Jack felt a sudden rage made stronger by its impotence.

He might not be able to slay the dragons of her past, he knew, but that didn't stop him from wanting to try and comfort her now. "Will you trust me to touch you?" She stared at him, obviously a bit surprised by the request. He didn't realize he'd held his breath until she dipped her chin in the barest of movements.

He ran his palm lightly over her hair, traced a finger along her cheek, then gently pulled her into his arms, pressing her cheek against his shoulder. She resisted at first, but he whispered in her ear, "It's okay, April. Let someone hold you. Let me hold you." He felt an incredible sense of joy when she slowly relaxed in his arms.

He suspected she needed to talk about it, maybe even wanted to. But he was loath to do anything to end this respite. He gently smoothed the loose strands of her hair, wanting desperately to know what she was thinking, remembering. What had her old man done to her? And what about her mother?

A dozen other questions popped into his mind and he silently cursed the inquisitive journalist that was as much a permanent part of him as his arms and legs. But he also knew his need to uncover and understand what had happened in her past went deeper than the basic instinct to get to the root of a story.

"If you ever want to talk about it, I'm here," he murmured against her hair, the soft fragrance enveloping him in a calming, soothing embrace. The slight tightening of her arms before she moved back was the only indication she gave that she'd heard him.

"I really should be getting back." Her voice was still hushed, as if she'd been sharing secrets meant for his ears only.

"April, wait."

She scooted to the edge of the couch and turned to face him again, her expression not quite the professional mask she was obviously struggling to wear.

"We still need to decide what to do about my fee."

She looked as if she'd been slapped. He'd wanted her to stay longer, so he'd said the most asinine thing in the world, guaranteed to make her think his holding her had been a calculated act. He hurried to do some damage control before she came out swinging.

"I didn't mean that the way it sounded. Honest. Forget the damn deal, okay?" He raked a hand through his hair in a gesture of frustration. Releasing a huge sigh, he looked at her. "I'm sorry. It's just that I want to spend some time with you."

He saw her anger falter a bit and stomped down a twinge of guilt for being about to seize that small opportunity. The most important thing right now was getting her to agree; he could kick himself for his methods later. Hell, if she said yes, he'd let *her* kick him.

"No cameras, okay? Just you and me taking a little time to escape the pressure." Her eyebrows furrowed as if she were debating the merits of his offer. "You pick the time, I'll provide the entertainment, and we'll call it even."

Her eyebrows raised as her eyes widened, and he couldn't help the laugh that escaped him at her obvious interpretation of what he'd meant by "entertainment." "Not that kind," he teased, grinning broadly. "But I'm glad to see we're back on the same wavelength."

That almost earned him a smile. Her lips quirked at the corners and he felt his heart do a double take. Yep, he was in serious trouble here.

"All right," she answered, still sounding a bit tentative. "But it will probably take a few days to schedule in some time. What kind of time frame did you have in mind?"

"I don't know. Whatever you can spare. Say, an afternoon? Surely the resort won't go to ruin if you take off for three or four hours."

Only one eyebrow lifted at that, but he got his smile. It was worth any and all amount of trouble and suffering.

"You'd be surprised what can happen around here in thirty minutes, much less three hours." When he started to speak, she raised her hand to stop him. "I'll do the best I can. Deal?" She lowered her hand and offered it to him.

"Absolutely." He took her hand in his and tugged it a little, forcing her to shift closer to him to keep her balance. Turning her palm upward, he kept his eyes locked on hers as he slowly lowered his mouth and pressed a soft kiss in the center of it. Then he slowly curled her fingers into her palm.

He raised his head; their eyes remained locked on each other. Long seconds elapsed as they searched each other's eyes. The total silence was both pulse-poundingly loud and infinitely peaceful.

Little by little, April's hand slid from his grasp. Praying her legs would hold her, she slowly rose from the couch, the action a bit awkward as she was unable to tear her gaze away from his. She backed into the coffee table, her calves bumping around the edge, then reluctantly turned toward the door.

She stepped into the blade of sunshine slicing through the slightly opened door, wondering why it no longer represented freedom to her. Instead it was as if the world on the other side of that door suddenly represented risk—the risk of failure, the risk of success, the risk of the past coming back to haunt her. Only here, in Jack's arms, had she felt safe, secure.

She thought of what Senator Smithson had told her and knew the greatest risk of all was still waiting for her. The risk of old, unwanted pain and humiliation finding her again and ruining everything she'd worked so hard for.

With one hand on the door, she turned to find

that Jack had risen and was watching her closely, the intensity of the moment they'd shared still reflected in his eyes.

If she stayed here, she instinctively knew Jack would protect her from the pain and humiliation, or at least he'd try. But who would protect her from the risk of a broken heart?

Jack stared at the door for several long minutes after April walked out into the afternoon sunshine. He downed the rest of his beer in one shot and pushed himself off the couch. He recalled again the stricken look in her eyes when he'd inadvertently called her by her father's pet name. He thought back to the wedding reception several days ago when he'd called her that.

Jack froze in mid-stride. She was pale and stiff then, too, but he hadn't been the cause. Smithson. What in the hell did Smithson have to do with April's father? Or her past?

Jack sat down on one of the wicker bar stools by the counter that separated the small kitchen from the dining area and pulled a pad of resort stationery in front of him. He jotted a few notes, mostly impressions of the Senator and April and the conversation between them that had precipitated his intervention.

He paused in his writing, tapping the pencil

against the paper. His instincts were running on full alert. The problem was that where April was concerned, he wasn't sure if his instincts were journalistic, or protective. Either way, he added another item to the mental to-do list he'd started the second April had left the bungalow.

One of those items was to find out what sort of communication equipment the resort had. He wanted to do some preliminary checking on the Senator.

But the first item on his list was making sure he was penciled into April's schedule as soon as possible. She hadn't been gone ten minutes and he already missed her.

"*Señor* Jack took care of it." April chanted the phrase for what had to be the twelfth time that morning. She was beginning to think it was the new resort slogan. The pattern had become alarmingly clear over the past forty-eight hours, and April ground her teeth in frustration.

"Is no problem, *sí*?" Antonio looked worried.

"No, no problem," April reassured him, holding in her sigh until Antonio flashed a smile and turned back to the other tables. After all, it wasn't the maitre d's fault if one of the guests, namely Jack, decided to take it upon himself to soothe the ruffled feathers of a fellow, or rather female, guest who'd become outraged when Antonio had inadvertently dumped an entire platter of freshly cut pineapple on her lap. Poor Antonio had probably been distracted by the same generous cleavage that had prompted Jack to come to the rescue.

Not that she cared in the least what he did or with whom, she just didn't like the way he'd managed to magically appear every time one of the guests, usually female, developed some urgent problem. He was supposed to be here relaxing, wasn't he?

She supposed she ought to be happy, ecstatic even, that he was putting his incredible charm to good use. Her daily agenda was impossible enough, and by taking care of those pesky but oh-so-important little squabbles that were routine in a resort this size, Jack had actually given her more time to concentrate on some of the weightier issues she faced. Like getting the outside landscaping firm she'd hired to agree to let the local Indians help with the actual physical labor.

April's frustration with Jack couldn't be averted even by that headache. She clenched and unclenched her fists. Several times. It didn't help. She still wanted to punch him, and she was a card-carrying pacifist, so she knew she was bordering on unreasonable. Hell, she acknowledged, adding a mumbled Mexican curse, she'd passed that point about three "*Señor* Jack took care of it's" ago.

She forced her hands to uncurl and laid them flat on the table beside her, wanting to sip her tea and pretend a calm she still didn't feel, but afraid she'd crush the delicate china. Face it, she told herself, what you're really angry about is the fact that you've spent a large part of the last two days reliving how great Jack's arms felt around you, relishing the feel of that hard, firm chest pressed against your cheek, and . . . oh hell, and that during the darkest part of those hours you wondered just what he'd taste like.

And Jack had apparently decided that his idea of fun was becoming a one-man customer relations squad. She didn't even want to speculate on what kind of relations he'd had with those customers—*her* customers!—that had so effectively kept the guests, at least the female ones, so unusually complaint-free for the last two days. She groaned and dropped her head into her palms.

She knew the second she was no longer alone, because the hairs on her neck lifted in the familiar way they did when Jack was anywhere in the vicinity. She'd had to accept this disturbing phenomenon as foolproof. Every time it had happened over the last two days, she'd looked up to find him nearby, usually talking to other guests, occasionally lining up intricate shots with his camera equipment. She wasn't sure why it bothered her so much that he'd made no effort to speak with her. He usually settled for a wave; at the most she got a smile and a quick nod.

It didn't matter, she thought, reminding herself how mad she was at him. She lifted her head slowly. Still foolproof. By now, however, he was much closer; he was sitting right across from her at the patio table where she'd been trying to eat lunch. She didn't trust herself to speak, so she settled for trying to burn holes through his damnably sexy, white polo shirt with her eyes.

"Have a minute? Mind if I join you?"

April opened her mouth and closed it again, then looked around to make sure most of the late lunchers had left the side patio before risking a response. Just to be on the safe side, she put her newly curled fists into her lap.

"You know perfectly well just how many free minutes I have and if you're here for a thank-you, then consider yourself thanked." She clutched at the linen napkin in her lap and tossed it on her uneaten lunch, rising at the same time. "I'm sorry if I seem abrupt, but I'm sure there are still one or two things that need my attention around here."

Jack fought his smile when she lifted one beautifully arched brow as if waiting for him to confirm or deny her assumption.

Highly underrated features, eyebrows. He wished he'd brought along his Nikon. But no, the glittering golden eyes below those lush brows made it crystal clear now was *not* the right time to suggest a photo opportunity. "Well, if you're not too busy, could you be persuaded to join me for lunch?"

She started to mention the obvious, but he silenced her by reaching over and lifting the napkin off of her still full plate.

"Pierre having an off day?"

April's lips twitched despite her fierce attempts to focus on her anger. She was still mad at him, but when his lips curved in that oh-so-innocent smile, she was hard put not to give up being angry and smile back.

Just to prove to him she couldn't be bought off with something as trifling as a sexy smile, she said, "If he were, I'm certain you'd have handled it by now."

His eyes widened as if she'd surprised him by continuing to snipe, then he ruined her triumph by actually having the gall to wink at her!

"Sorry, *señorita*, Pierre's on his own. I pack my own lunch."

April leaned over the table to glance at the ground near his chair. Nothing. As if guessing the direction of her thoughts, he raised his hands. Both were empty.

"I wasn't sure if you'd come, so I left the basket back in my bungalow."

April actually snorted. Very unladylike, but under the circumstances, highly appropriate.

"What was that for?"

"You expect me to believe you've been running around playing majordomo for the past two days just to be turned down after all your hard work?"

"You've heard the 'lunch basket in my bungalow' routine before, huh?" His green eyes twinkled and his smile split into a full grin. "Damn, and I thought my plan was foolproof."

April couldn't have prevented the smile curving her lips for all the tortillas in Mexico. "Win some, lose some." She tried for a casual shrug, but Jack had skirted the table and taken her hand in his before she could blink.

He leaned and whispered in her ear. "I guess I'll have to resort to plan B."

April conceded defeat, forcing herself to admit it hadn't left even a trace of bitterness in her mouth. "Okay, I'll bite. What's plan B?"

Jack tugged her hand a little harder and started out across the lawn, heading toward the guest bungalows. "Did I ever mention that one of my ancestors was a pirate?"

She laughed despite herself. She had no trouble picturing a swashbuckling Jack, complete with black eye patch. "No. And what does that have to do with plan B?"

"Kidnapping. A family tradition."

April's step faltered a bit, but Jack just tightened his grip and steered her around the tall hedge-row separating the lawn from the paths that wove throughout the resort compound.

"And did your ancestors kidnap unwilling women and hold them prisoner on their own ships? Unwise move, don't you think?"

Between one breath and the next Jack pivoted and pulled her into the shady seclusion of the jaca-randa trees. He turned so his back was facing the path, sheltering her from view. He gently pulled her closer, then draped her arms across his shoulders and linked his hands behind her waist.

Locking his gaze on hers, he said quietly, "Who said the women were unwilling?"

April didn't answer. His heated voice made her think of sizzling, sun-filled days and steamy tropical nights. She knew from the heightened intensity of his gaze that she'd already incriminated herself.

"Are you willing, April? Say yes. I spent two whole days being a good boy, but if I have to spend one more second wondering what you taste like, I'm likely to disgrace my forebears right here in the woods."

Fleeting thoughts of where she was and how she should be behaving became a memory as his raspy plea vibrated through her. His quiet humor enchanted her, relaxing her in ways she hadn't allowed herself the luxury of in years. But it was the glitter of desire electrifying his light green eyes that created a need in her so strong nothing else could compete with it.

"Is this taste test part of your lunch menu?" Feeling anything but casual with him, she tried to match his whimsical humor, but feared the quiver in her voice betrayed her need.

His ragged sigh bolstered her confidence.

"An appetizer. Only an appetizer."

He unlinked his hands, shifting her more tightly against him with the arm that was still wrapped around her waist, and using the other hand to slowly twine a stray curl around his finger. Keeping his eyes locked on hers, looking at her with such intensity she thought she'd simply ignite if he didn't kiss her soon, he leaned closer until his lips almost brushed hers.

"I need you to do one thing for me."

Surprised at the request, but somehow thrilled at the prospect of being needed by him, she wet her lips and answered, "What?"

"Kiss me first. I have to know you want this as much as I do."

April answered with the first thing that entered her mind. "Gladly." She tightened her fingers, which had somehow managed to work their way into the thick hair curling at his nape, and gently tugged his head down until she could lift up on her toes and reach his lips with her own.

His lips were softer than she'd thought possible, like warm velvet. She probed gently at first, reveling in the musky taste that was him. A small part of her realized he was holding himself perfectly still during her exploration, and she began to think her rusty attempts had turned him off.

She started to pull back, only to feel the arm behind her back tighten. He lifted a hand to cradle the back of her head and her motions stilled as she felt the slight trembling of his fingers as he wove them through her hair.

"That's right, April. Don't ever doubt your effect on me."

Her hands slid down from his shoulders and neck to clutch at the front of his white shirt. She tore her gaze away from his and tried to focus on the dark blond swirl of hair peeking from the opened buttons at his neck, but the feel of his heart pounding under her fingers proved a greater distraction.

Jack watched her pupils dilate even further as she caressed the fabric stretched over his heart. Sweet mercy, she was going to kill him right here.

"April, *mi corazón*, you can study the fine Korean craftsmanship of my shirt later." She looked up at him, confusion clearly written on her face. "Is it my turn yet?" he asked.

April had no idea how he managed to blend fierce protectiveness, intense desire, and a trace of raw vulnerability in that one look. She barely managed to nod yes.

FIVE

April held her breath as Jack lowered his head, her eyes slowly closing. A second later she opened them again. "Jack?"

He studied her in silence for another second, then said, "Not here." He gently lifted her arms from his neck, but captured one of her hands as he turned to leave their shaded hideaway. He guided her onto the path, then loosened his grip but didn't drop her hand completely. "Meet me at my bungalow in about ten minutes, okay?"

April knew she looked as confused as she felt. "What? Why?" Her brows furrowed in the beginnings of anger. "I thought the game playing was over. If this is your idea of a jo—"

Jack gently squeezed her hand, then dropped

it. "What this is, is my idea of protecting your reputation as boss of this joint."

"You didn't seem too concerned about that when you dragged me across the lawn," she shot back, partly angry, but mostly frustrated. She didn't have to admit that the frustration was mostly sexual in nature; she could hardly deny it. "I'm not just boss here, I own 'this joint,' as you so quaintly refer to it. And if I want to be seen holding hands or doing anything else with a guest then it's nobody's business but my own."

Jack looked surprised, then a wide smile split his tanned features. "So, you make a habit of this, then?" He ducked her halfhearted punch, but caught her fist, his big hand completely encompassing hers. He didn't pull her closer, but the intimacy reflected in his eyes effectively erased the distance. "I still want you to give me a few minutes' head start."

"If you're worried about your housekeeping, I've seen it, remember?" she said dryly.

Jack actually groaned, and groaned again when she arched that brow at him. "I'm trying to be a gentleman here, but you're making it hard." He gave a short laugh at his unintentional double entendre and turned her hand so he could lace his fingers with hers. "Which is precisely why I want a few minutes alone."

"Why now? A second ago I could have sworn—"

His voice quieted to a whisper. "Do you have

any idea what I wanted to do to you under that tree? What I would have done if I'd started kissing you?"

April felt a surge of heat and something like pride course through her. She'd put that look of wanting, of desire, on his face. It shocked her. It also thrilled her. "Probably the exact same thing I was hoping you'd do."

Jack swore and dropped her hand like he'd been burned. "Fifteen minutes, April." His voice was strained. "I swear, lunch was my original intention, my only intention. But if I see you any earlier, we go straight to dessert. Understand?"

Empowered by his reaction to her, April merely smiled. Forcing back the grin that teased the corners of her mouth, she nodded, then watched him retreat down the path, his long-legged, smooth stride covering the ground quickly.

April turned around and faced the lodge, blotting the image of those intense green eyes from her mind, trying to focus on what had really just happened. She should probably be embarrassed by her behavior, she belatedly realized. But she wasn't. Being aggressive was nothing new to her—building this resort had made that trait a necessity. But then this wasn't business, she argued with herself. This was personal.

And in that respect, she had to admit her reaction was way out of the ordinary. In fact, she'd never done anything like it before. After her pride had been destroyed during the harassment trial, April had shied away from all relationships. Gradually she'd learned to trust again, but by then building the resort had taken over her life. Her immediate reaction to Jack had taken some getting used to.

The grin she'd been suppressing slowly spread across her face. Jack Tango liked being in control. She perfectly understood that need. She hadn't had much chance to put it into practice relationship-wise, but she'd vowed the day she decided to come forward with her charges against Markham that any relationship she did have would be equal risk and aboveboard—with no chance of one person holding the upper hand. It was the only way to remain safe.

Safe. That word didn't seem to fit Jack. Always cool, sexy, and so damned sure of his charm. But unless she was completely off the mark, her little speech just now had actually made Jack Tango nervous.

The very idea made her skin tingle.

Jack punched his key card into the lock slot on the bungalow door. Once inside he went directly to the kitchen. He methodically began sorting through the contents of the basket he'd packed earlier, forcing himself to concentrate on making sure he hadn't forgotten anything. It was no use.

He slammed the wicker lid down and paced around the room. After several paths to the window and back he collapsed onto the small couch.

No matter how he tried, he couldn't reconcile the troubled, skittish woman he'd comforted in his arms on this very couch two days ago with the sexy, confident lady who'd looked into his eyes not five minutes ago and basically stated she wanted him as badly as he wanted her.

He was having a hard enough time figuring out what to do with all these new protective feelings she inspired in him. He'd known from the moment he'd decided to pursue her she'd need the kid-glove treatment. Something was eating at her, and he knew he'd better damn sure take it slow if he wanted to keep her from shutting him out. So what in the Sam Hill was she doing telling him it was okay to all but make love to her under a tree in broad daylight for chrissakes?

Jack groaned and let his head drop back on the edge of the couch. "Women." Minutes later he opened his eyes and stared at the ceiling. "Franklin, you owe me for this one."

"What does Franklin have to do with this?"

Jack snapped his head up. April was standing in the doorway. "How did you get in here? Never mind, stupid question," he added, seeing the master card in her hand. It bothered him that he'd some-how lost the upper hand.

"Have a seat." She lifted her brow just slightly at his curt command, but she moved to sit down, choosing a seat across from him. Very telling. He smiled. Apparently her assertiveness had faded somewhat, along with the arousal. Good.

"Who is Franklin?"

"A friend. Colleague, actually." Jack's response was automatic. He was busy watching the light play across her hair, deciding which filter would be most flattering. Nah, she didn't need any help, she'd photograph beautifully under even the harshest light.

"I remember you blaming him earlier, when I first met you. For being here, I mean. Does it have something to do with your job?"

Jack dragged his attention back to the conversation. He propped his feet up on the coffee table, telling himself he was glad she was providing them both with a reprieve. The new position didn't ease his discomfort, but maybe he could at least hide his condition from her view.

Reprieve or not, her deep, steady voice made it difficult to forget there was a big queen-size bed in the next room. "My job?" he answered, hoping he remembered the question. "Well, sort of. I guess you could say I tend to be a bit aggressive about my work. Somehow I let Franklin manage to convince me that taking a few weeks off would not bring the world to a grinding halt."

"So, is it Franklin's choice of Mexico? Or Paradise Cove? Or do you just miss working and want to get back?"

Jack stopped restlessly tapping his feet together and looked directly at her. Judging from her earnest expression, she wasn't just making idle chitchat, she really seemed to want to know. "It's partly being stuck so far away from anything without there being a real purpose for it," he said quietly. "It's partly the feeling that I should be working on another assignment."

"So you don't miss it as much as you thought you would?"

Jack stilled completely, his gaze pinned on hers. Her ability to cut to the core of things still startled him. She heard things he hadn't been aware of saying. Until she'd asked, even he hadn't acknowledged that a large part of the unsettling disquiet plaguing him since he'd arrived here was due to exactly that possibility.

He ignored for now the myriad of questions her comment provoked him to consider. Instead he finished answering her earlier question. "But the main reason I was swearing at Franklin when you walked in was because if it wasn't for him, I wouldn't have met you."

April's eyes widened and she stiffened in the chair. "I wasn't aware I'd made such a nuisance out of myself."

Jack leaned forward, swung his feet to the floor, and stood, his motions controlled and fluid. He stepped around the low table separating them. April immediately got up and moved several feet away. Jack halted, his light eyes glittering as they narrowed. "I'd think by now you'd know I'm not going to do anything that isn't a mutual decision."

The hurt he'd felt at her retreat lessened considerably when she squared her shoulders and held her ground as he moved to stand in front of her. It took guts, he knew, to try to stare down a man a good foot taller than herself. "I've been very careful to go slowly with you." He felt his lips twitch at the disbelief that crossed her face. "I haven't done anything without your consent, have I?"

"If you're not counting the pictures you took of me at the reception, no."

"The pictures aren't the issue here." He stepped closer and felt his body warm as he confirmed that the look in her eyes was one of irritation, not fear. He'd never been more turned on, or more confused, in his whole life. "I want to get to know you. Spend time with you. After what happened under that tree you can hardly deny it's only one-sided."

"I wanted you to kiss me back, if that's what you mean. But I don't like being made to feel guilty that you're attracted to me. I didn't like being attracted to you either; it's confusing and I wasn't planning on it. But, at least once I admitted it to myself,

I was honest with you about it. I don't know if anything will ever happen between us, but I won't sneak around to find out."

She was so damn direct it unnerved him. Jack felt as if he were teetering on the edge of a giant, gaping crevasse, tiptoeing along the rim. One wrong move and he'd be swept away forever. "I wasn't trying to hide anything by bringing you here. I was under the misguided impression you would prefer to continue what we started out there in private. And for the record, you can't plan everything in life."

He placed his hands on her hips; the gentle thrust of her hipbones pressing against his big hands made him aware of just how much bigger he was than her. She didn't try to move or shift away and he gave in to the need to feel her against him. He pulled her closer and slowly shifted her back and forth, his arousal unmistakable against her flat belly.

"You want honesty? This is what you do to me every time you look at me, talk to me. Even when you're mad at me. I don't like feeling this way either, April. I don't like not being in control. But I'm not hiding from it, either."

April reached up to grip Jack's shoulders for support, barely drawing enough breath to fill her lungs. His body was hot and hard against hers and she had a sudden desperate need for him to lift her up so that his erection would be pressed against the ache between her legs instead of being wasted against her stomach. "Jack?" Her voice was a low rasp.

"What, *mi tesoro*?"

My treasure. The endearment was at once rough with need and tender with concern.

"I do want you." She gasped as he groaned and gripped her hips tighter, pressing himself more deeply against her. "But, I think . . ." She looked down at their bodies. How wonderful it felt to finally be this close to him. "I may hate myself for this."

Jack shifted his arm behind her back so he could tilt her chin with his finger until she looked him in the eyes. "No regrets, April. But stop me now if you don't intend to finish this."

"I want to eat lunch first."

"What?" His tone was the epitome of disbelief. "*Now* you're hungry? For food?"

"No, not in the least."

"You're not the only one confused here, lady."

She reached up a trembling finger, pressing it against his lips. "I meant it, what I said earlier. I just need to go a bit slower. Does it have to be all or nothing?"

Jack blew out a deep breath, struggling with his need for her, to be on top of her, inside of her. He let his finger trail along the side of her jaw. "It shouldn't be, no. I've known you less than a week and yet it's taking every bit of my willpower not to tug you down on this tile floor, lift that skirt to your hips, and do everything I can think of to make you beg me to be deep inside of you."

He watched her pupils expand as he spoke until the brown was almost swallowed by her black irises. He was fascinated by the convulsing of the muscles in her slender throat as she tried to come to terms with her body's response to his words. His gaze dropped lower and he had to forcibly restrain himself from lowering his lips to the tightened nipples straining against her thin blouse.

"Pretty amazing, isn't it?" His voice was deep and dark.

"You have no idea," she finally choked out. With that cryptic statement, April eased out of his arms and walked to the kitchen.

Jack let her go, very unwillingly, but knowing she'd been right to put a halt on things. She wasn't the only one who felt out of her depth. He cleared his throat and followed her into the tiny kitchen, leaning against the bar. "If you still want to, I sorta thought we could eat on the beach. I figured you'd know all the secluded spots." She darted a quick look at him and he added, "And the crowded ones."

"I think we'd better stick to the public beach."

Jack relaxed as she smiled, her tone dry, her voice even. He grinned, allowing himself to switch back to the comfortable charm he used to keep people at a distance, and winked. "Just remember,

I still haven't had my turn at kissing yet. Are you sure you want to risk it?"

He was close enough now to see the quick flare of desire darken her brown eyes before she looked away, and he cursed himself for teasing her. He also made a mental note to start wearing baggier shorts around her. "Don't answer that." He grabbed the basket. "I'll haul the food, you tote the blanket. Deal?"

"Deal." She scooped up the woven cotton blanket and he stepped aside to let her pass. She headed out the door and down the path without looking back.

April glanced briefly at her watch, then turned her attention back to the action on the beach. She couldn't believe she'd been playing hooky for two hours. Thoughts of what she should be doing skittered away as she watched Jack's bare chest expand and the muscles of his arm bunch as he soared into the air and slammed the volleyball down over the net. The referee called a foul and April leapt to her feet, yelling and pumping her fist with the rest of the sizeable crowd.

It wasn't until she heard herself threatening to fire the ref unless he reversed the call that she realized what she was doing. She cast a quick glance around, but no one was paying any attention to her.

All eyes were riveted on the match, as they had been for most of the last hour.

With a sheepish smile, she plopped back down on the blanket and fiddled with the last piece of mango. After a quiet lunch of tuna salad, fresh fruit, and light, impersonal talk, Jack had offered a walk on the beach. April had declined. Not because she didn't want to go; she wanted to go very badly. But she'd started to wonder if maybe Jack had been right about keeping their combustive reaction to each other behind closed doors. He'd been a total gentleman during lunch, yet her pulse hadn't slowed down one bit.

She was still intent on keeping everything open and aboveboard, but since she wasn't sure she could hold his hand for a quiet walk without tugging him into the first empty cabana she saw to finish that kiss, she'd declined. He'd smiled and taken it gracefully. She hadn't been sure how she felt about that, but since the volleyball game had started right after, she hadn't had much time to dwell on it. She'd pooped out after the first match, but Jack had continued playing.

She watched his team score on another of his spectacular spikes, then turned to gather up the picnic supplies. As much as she'd appreciated the opportunity to ogle Jack's hard-muscled physique to her heart's content for the last hour, she had to get back to work.

She didn't want to disrupt the game, but she didn't want to just leave either. She stood and brushed the sand from the white shorts she'd changed into after leaving the bungalow, then felt a warm hand grip her elbow. She tensed as she looked up, but relaxed as she gazed into the now-familiar translucent green eyes.

"Playtime's over, huh?" His voice was a bit gravelly from exertion, and it had no small effect on her system.

"For me, yes." She smiled, squinting into the sun. "You go ahead and finish the game, though."

Jack's eyes widened in surprise. His large frame blocked out the game, but not the other players' voices as they called him to come back. He glanced back at them, then at her. "You're serious, aren't you?"

"You *are* on vacation. I can find my way to my office. Go, have fun." She didn't add that she thought he could use a bit of mindless fun in his life. But the look in his eyes told her she didn't have to.

"You're sure?"

"Consider it a direct order from the CEO."

A grin split his tanned face and he closed the space between them, shielding her completely from view. "I love it when you order me around. I *will* see you later."

"I'll probably be working late tonight." At the frown that creased his brow she added, "Even *Señor* Jack can't solve all of the Cove's problems in a day or two. Speaking of which, you should relax and enjoy what the Cove has to offer."

"I thought I was." April moved back slightly, but Jack reached out to hold her arm in a gentle grip. His voice was low and carried only as far as her ears. He didn't hide his frustration. "I didn't mean that like it sounded. If I truly thought you were just one of the Cove's perks, I sure as hell would have worked off the sexual energy we built up in a much more enjoyable way than playing volleyball in ninety-plus heat."

April's eyes widened, causing Jack to smile again.

"You mean that's why you . . . ?"

"Yeah. For a whole hour. And if you keep looking at me like that, I'm gonna have to do laps next." The shouts for Jack to return grew louder, but he kept his gaze on her. "You'll be in your office later?"

"Yes, except for a few minutes before the nightly show. I usually greet the guests just before showtime and make several announcements about upcoming events."

"Did you mean what you said earlier?"

April looked confused, then wary. "Probably. Which thing?"

"About not sneaking around."

"I'm here on the beach with you, aren't I?"

Jack's grin broadened to a bright white smile. "Yeah, I guess you are. Then you won't mind if I do this."

Before she could answer, he pulled her into his arms and pressed his lips to hers. His kiss was hard, hot, and over entirely too soon.

"It was my turn, right?" he whispered in her ear.

April nodded mutely, but the whistles of a few of the guests brought her back to the present. A volleyball landed in a spray of sand at his feet and he stepped away. He toed the ball up into his hands and looked back at her.

She could have sworn that for a split second he'd been searching her face for signs he'd acted out of line. He hadn't been. After all, she'd given him the green light earlier, under the tree. She smiled back at him and his cocky grin instantly surfaced.

He backed his way toward the net, his eyes flashing, a teasing smile on his face, popping the ball onto his biceps like a beach bum trying to impress his girl.

She couldn't resist. She flashed him a big smile and said in a clear voice, "See you later, Moondoggie." She had the satisfaction, as she climbed up the stairs leading from the beach to the grounds, of hearing the other men razz Jack.

She grinned all the way to her office, amazed that she'd spent the afternoon behaving like a college kid on spring break, at her own resort no less! Her smile faltered as images of the far more mature activity she could have spent the steamy afternoon indulging in floated through her mind.

April entered her office and sat down behind her desk. The large room was a dozen degrees cooler than the beach, yet she felt hotter, uncomfortable.

Forcing the tantalizing images from her mind, she swiveled her chair and looked out the large window to the beach below. She didn't bother to kid herself that she wasn't hoping for a glimpse of him. She could see the volleyball game from here, but not enough to tell which one was Jack. She had no doubt she'd see him again tonight. The thought sent a thrill of anticipation through her.

Jack may have seemed more relaxed on the beach, but she knew it would take more than a volleyball game to truly unwind the tension and weariness that lay beneath the surface of his charming smile. It went far deeper than corporate burnout. Getting involved with Jack would not be light and easy. But nothing in her life, good or bad, had ever been either of those things. All that remained to be seen was which category having a relationship with him would fall in to.

Jack crossed the moonlit lawn, enjoying the cooler midnight air. The grass was cool and wet between his toes and the evening wind whipped the dampness from his freshly showered hair. As he neared the entrance to the main building, he shifted the cooler in his hand and glanced down at the baggy chinos and print shirt he wore as he slipped on the beach thongs he's bought earlier at the Cove's gift shop.

He had a sudden wild urge to go back to the bungalow and put on something less . . . rumpled. A wry smile crossed his face. Since when had he cared how he dressed? Besides, April had already seen him wearing less.

His thoughts drifted to how she'd stared at him the day he'd caught her looking through the reception pictures. He'd only been wearing a bath towel, but at the time had been grateful for the coverage, considering his immediate response to her.

Now he paused and looked up at the windows at the top of the half dozen of so floors. Yellow light blinked between the slats of the blinds of a large corner office that wrapped around the back of the building. He headed into the lobby.

He immediately spotted the concierge. Surprised that he was still on duty, Jack nodded to the dark-skinned man, then abruptly headed over to him. "*Buenas noches*, Dominguez," he said in greeting.

"*Hola, Señor* Jack. What can I do for you?" He nodded to the small cooler Jack held in one hand.

Jack looked down as if wondering what had caught Dom's attention. "Oh," he answered, then glanced back up, "nothing right now. But I'm expecting some mail in the next few days. I'd really appreciate it if you could get it to me as soon as it comes in."

"*Sí, sí*. No problem." He grinned at Jack and nodded, flashing one gold-capped tooth.

Jack nodded back, then paused a moment, suddenly realizing that he felt uncomfortable about going to the lobby elevator. His destination would be all too clear to Dom and anyone else who cared to watch the illuminating numbers above the lobby doors as he rode to the top floor.

It was ridiculous. He'd never felt the need, or even had an urge, to protect the reputation of the women he'd dated. They'd all been sophisticated and intelligent enough to be responsible for their decisions. Which made the urge to protect April all the more confusing. Jack smiled briefly at Dom and moved a few steps away in the general direction of the elevator.

More than any of the other women he'd dated, April, with her achievements, certainly knew her own mind. He paced over to the gleaming brass doors, his finger hovering over the arrow button. So why, he silently asked himself, especially in light of the statements she'd made to him that very afternoon, were his instincts still screaming at him to go slow, to protect, to take special care?

Because, his mind responded, beneath that competent, efficient CEO face she presented to the world, a fragile layer existed, one he suspected she'd rarely allowed anyone to see. But he had seen it, had held her while she came to grips with whatever had caused it.

Jack shook off the questions shooting through his mind. Chances were good that he'd get his answers in the information he'd requested. Until then, there was no point dwelling on the reasons, when his time could be much better spent getting to know everything about April on a firsthand basis.

Resisting the urge to glance back to see if Dom was watching, Jack punched the "up" arrow. It would be foolish to even try to conceal his destination. Hotels were the same all over the world. The up-to-the-second information available through their grapevines had saved his butt more than a few times. By now the kiss on the beach was certainly old news.

The doors slid silently open and he stepped inside and turned around. Not a soul was paying the least bit of attention to him. Jack smiled as the doors slid shut. April's staff was well trained—efficient and, more important, discreet.

Once on the top floor, Jack headed toward the office that he'd noticed from down on the lawn. Cracking open the door, he stepped into an outer office. Glad that April didn't have employees with her workaholic tendencies, he slipped past the unoccupied secretary's desk and quietly leaned over to peek into the partly open door leading to her office.

He'd expected to see her at her desk, her dark head bent over a pile of paperwork. What he saw instead took his breath away and rooted him to the spot.

She stood with her back to him, gazing out the huge picture window behind her desk. Her silk caramel-colored dress was backless. He let his gaze drift down the delicate ridge of her spine exposed by the loose halter style, then rest for a moment on the narrow gold belt circling her waist. The slight flare of her hips could barely be seen above the low back of her chair. His pulse pounded when she shifted her weight slightly and a sigh whispered through her lips.

His hand went immediately to his chest, groping for the nonexistent camera. His need to capture the essence of this moment forever on film hit him so hard he had to clench his fingers in a fist to keep from pounding them on the door frame in frustration.

So he did the next best thing and allowed the impact of her to flow over and through him. He responded fully to the moment, to her, wanting to enjoy the rush while it lasted. He had an insane desire to trace his tongue along the length of her too-rigid spine, then slip his hands in the sides of her loose top. His skin tightened as he flexed his muscles against the response his body had to thoughts of how her small breasts would feel in his large hands, what they would look like, taste like.

He must have made a sound, because she whirled around, one small hand clutching the very spot he'd been imagining his hand touching.

"Jack! You scared me to death."

She'd been a million miles away, but the startled look on her face made it clear her thoughts hadn't been of him. Jack yanked his eyes from the silky fabric clutched in her hands and the way it pulled the fabric tight over her obviously braless breasts. It took a moment longer to regain his voice. "Sorry." The word was barely more than a rasp.

April fell silent, simply staring at him. He did the same. She lowered her hand as his gaze traveled over her.

He wished the front of her dress plunged deeply like the back. The gathered silk that fastened tight at her neck kept him from discovering if her pulse was pounding as rapidly as his. Nonetheless, he found it next to impossible to pull his gaze away from that slender neck and focus on her eyes.

Surprise had been replaced by an open look of desire that rocked him to his knees. To look at her now—chin firm, those almond-shaped eyes meeting his gaze head-on—he couldn't believe he had spent one second worrying about protecting her. Hers was the face of a woman who knew exactly what she wanted.

In a reflex gesture he lifted the cooler in his hand. "Hungry?"

She didn't even glance at the cooler. "Famished."

Jack stepped into the office and closed the door.

SIX

"What are you doing here this late?" April's voice was lower, huskier.

"I might ask you the same question. But I won't." Jack moved to her desk and put the cooler down on one of the chairs. April remained behind the desk. "I told you I'd see you again. Are you really so surprised?"

Until that moment April would have denied just how badly she had wanted to believe he would find her here. That she'd prolonged leaving for just that possibility. Now that he stood not two feet from her she could feel her entire body responding to him, the mere sight of him, the sound of his voice. She didn't even try to deny it. "No, I suppose not."

Jack moved around the desk. At the last second

April turned back to face the window, afraid she'd do something foolish. Like rub her body wantonly against him just to feel the satiny material of her dress scrape across her bare breasts as she pressed them against his hard-muscled chest.

His breath was warm on her neck as he moved behind her. She held her breath, wanting to scream from the intensity of the desire mounting in her body, knowing she would if he didn't touch her. Quickly. All over. "Jack?" His name was a hoarse rasp, barely discernible even to her own ears.

"What do you want, April?"

Her only response, the only one she was capable of, was a shiver that ran the length of her spine and made her inner thighs quiver. She heard the soft rustle of fabric and then a click that plunged the office into darkness. The moonlight pouring through the open blinds provided surreal lighting.

"Do you want me to touch you, *mi tesoro?*"

Jack's breath was warm on the skin beneath her ear. She nodded.

"Do you know that you affect me like no other woman? I'm intrigued by you, your control, your sensuality. Even when I arrived here half dead with fatigue, you got to me."

Jack's words were more excruciating than any caress and April thought she'd die from the mixture of wonder and need that laced his rough tone. *Please touch me*, she wanted to scream out loud. But she trembled in silence, wanting to hear only his voice in the darkness as he orally stroked her.

His body was so close to her now she could feel his heat on her bare back; the slight brush of his shirt against her skin was almost unbearably sensitizing.

"Yet, I can't figure you out," he went on relentlessly, his voice even deeper now. "Something has forced you to hide your responsive nature. You maintain such a careful distance. And yet you respond to me. Totally. Why, April?"

She didn't answer, unwilling to say the words he wanted to hear, needed to hear. She wished he'd keep talking. But he remained damnably silent.

On a choked whisper, she finally said, "Because I can't *not* respond to you."

She felt him withdraw from her and fought the urge to cry out and beg him to return. She wanted him to bury himself deep inside her, not make her face the reasons she wanted him. She dropped her head forward against the blinds.

"Not good enough, April." His gentle tone belied a controlled anger. "I want you. Here. Now. On the desk. On the floor. Up against the damn wall. But it's you I want. Specifically, totally, and without regret. I think you want all that, too. Except for that last part."

He abruptly moved up behind her until his body came into contact with the back of her body—

enough contact to make his desire for her an absolute certainty. "I need that last part. No regrets."

April had already come to the conclusion that they would make love, when she'd kissed him under the jacaranda tree. But she now knew it wouldn't just be a physical joining, slaking only desire. No. He knew her too well. Yet, there was so much he didn't know. This wouldn't be simple or easy.

He would leave in a few weeks, but in that moment she knew she'd be the richer for having given her all to him—and, in return, having received all he would give to her. "No regrets," she said softly, honestly. Her spine remained straight, though, still not giving in to the need to lean into him, to let him take the last of her control away.

"I know something, someone made you doubt yourself. I just don't want any doubt between you and me, okay?" He punctuated his question by pressing a heartbreakingly gentle kiss on the sensitive skin at her nape.

He understood. Beyond reason he understood, and April knew he would care for her—body, mind, and soul—as no one else ever had. Or ever could. His intuitiveness was as powerful a stimulant as his body and his words. She melted.

Jack groaned. "Don't come undone on me yet, sweetheart. I'm so hungry for you it will take a while to work it all off." He pulled the ebony stick holding up her hair, letting the shiny waves caress his face as he buried his lips under her ear. "I need to see you." He pulled her pliant body back against his chest and reached for the cords that operated the blinds. He pulled them all the way up, bathing them in the glow of the three-quarter moon.

Wrapping his arms around her waist, he nuzzled her neck, willing himself to slow his need to take her immediately. He wanted to revel in her every breath, her every sigh. God, he wanted to pull her underneath him on the cold, hard floor. He took another deep breath of her sweet scent, the hint of muskiness rising from her skin burning his senses. Using everything he had in him he pulled the remainder of his control together, only to have her wrench it away completely with two words.

"Touch me."

He bit his inner cheek. Hard. "If I do, I won't stop. Not until every inch of your skin knows the feel of me."

"Yes."

No longer trusting speech, Jack moved trembling fingers up the length of her arms to her shoulders, then slid them slowly down along the sides of her halter dress. The high neckline, tight at the throat, covered her completely, yet provided the tantalizing freedom to slip his fingers in at the sides and across her breasts. She inhaled swiftly as he cupped her fullness and whispered softly in her ears. "So soft and sweet."

Still holding the light weight of her in his palms, he gently rubbed long fingers across her nipples. Her breath came in small gasps then, and Jack was rocked by the knowledge that his need for her could actually intensify. Fiercely maintaining his control, he continued to gently manipulate her breasts, and was rewarded when they became fuller and firmer in his large hands.

Tempering the urge to use his teeth to tear open the buttoned neckline of her dress, he forced himself to release her breasts. But his hands never left her warm skin as he slid his fingers back along the edge of her top and lifted her hair. "I want you to see my hands on you." He released the pearl buttons at her nape and her top fell to her waist, her dress held on only by her slim belt.

"Sweet heaven, are you beautiful." Jack nestled his chin on April's shoulder and whispered in her ear. "Look down. Watch my hands cover you." He moved his thumbs in slow circles around her hardened nipples as he spoke, evoking small gasps and a light shudder. "So small and perfect."

April couldn't remain silent any longer. "So large and gentle." When he paused, she covered his large hands with her smaller ones and he continued to caress her. The sweetness of his lovemaking, the eroticism of his words, made her feel almost removed from herself, yet more in touch within herself than she'd ever been, or could hope to be again. Except with him.

She watched the moonlight create shadows under his palms as he cupped her and whispered in her ear all the places she was going to watch him touch her. Small moans passed her lips unheeded. She was beyond coherent thought, responding to the purely primal demands of her body.

"Turn around. Touch me." She did as he asked and he cursed the shadows that deprived him of seeing her. Lifting her onto the small windowsill, he pressed her back against the cool glass, inhaling her gasp into his mouth. He pulled her arms around his neck as he pressed his tongue deep between her open lips. He tasted her, all of her.

Their tongues dueling, then thrusting until he groaned, he pushed her skirt to her hips and pulled her legs around his hips. Finding the strength to leave her mouth he whispered, "Don't let me go," then moved to taste her breasts.

She whimpered and bucked against him as he drew first one nipple, then the other into his hot mouth and drew them out to their fullest. "Take off my shirt," he commanded roughly. "I want to feel you against my chest."

April was half out of her mind by then and all but tore the shirt from his body. Once he was bared, she didn't pull him back into her arms. She couldn't. Not yet. First she wanted to—had to—taste him the way he had her. Inch by slow, wet inch.

She felt the tremors race across his skin and thrilled in the knowledge that he was dancing on the edge too. She moved to the pulse point along the side of his neck, which was erotically illuminated by the moonlight. She pressed a soft kiss on the very spot that pulsed, then ran her tongue over it before gently biting it. Abruptly Jack yanked his upper body away from her, his chest rising and falling in deep, rapid breaths.

Jerked halfway back to reality, April's mind swam for a moment and she spoke the first thought she had. "Did I hurt you?"

"Never, *mi cielo*." He paused to take several deep breaths, completely unaware of the name he'd used or of the fact that her eyes came into sharp and complete focus almost immediately. "But if your hot little tongue had wet so much as another inch of my skin, I couldn't have gotten my pants off in time to get inside you."

April felt pummeled, confused by the hard reality of his words and her body's continued response to them. Nonetheless, the endearment had thrown her, knocking her out of their syncopated rhythm. She felt lost, cheated, angry. But why? It was just a stupid nickname.

"April?"

The word was a combination query and demand. As in tune to her as she was to him, he had to know she'd pulled away too, in mind if not in body. She felt a hot burning beneath her eyelids and pressed them shut to keep the tears from falling.

All the beauty and passion that had built up to near bursting, only to be robbed of completion, of a satisfaction that would have fulfilled needs she'd never been aware of having. "I'm sorry." It was a wild understatement.

She felt his finger under her chin and spent all of a second trying to resist the slight pressure. She started to speak as she lifted her chin. "It isn't that I don't—" Her words died as she looked into his eyes. Totally devoid of color in the lunar light, they pierced her heart. "—want you," she finished softly, in awe of the intensity with which he looked at her, into her, into the very soul of her. And as quickly as that she was back on the edge.

"You touched me, kissed me, and..." He stopped, his voice giving out. He looked over her shoulder toward the distant waves.

For a long moment she remained silent. He seemed to be slipping away from her and she wondered if she'd imagined the wonder in his voice. She tightened her legs, which were still around his waist, and he moved against her immediately. This time she reached up and turned his chin toward her.

"I know. And somehow you were already deeper inside of me than anyone has ever been."

His eyes exploded in color as black pupils swallowed up the translucent irises in a savage wave of desire. She gulped at the naked hunger that drove into her like a physical thing, then without hesitation pulled him back toward her, needing to be what he wanted, to give what he needed. And more than anything, to be a part of the powerful force that was Jack.

"Nothing and no one can ever, ever compare to what you just gave me." Jack had barely ground out the words before he claimed her lips in a punishing kiss that he instinctively knew she would return fully. She gave all of it back and more. "Hold on tight," he ordered against her lips.

She clamped her thighs tightly and held on to his shoulders as he lifted her in his arms. He turned to her desk, but there was no place to put her down. She started to press small hot kisses on his neck and he looked wildly around her office, hoping for a couch or even a soft rug. Nothing but cold tile and narrow padded chairs met his gaze.

Her breasts crushed against him, she started nipping gently at the skin stretched across his shoulders, and he knew he would lose his mind if he didn't have her now. But it was when she pulled his earlobe into her sweet little mouth that he went out of control.

In one broad stroke he swept the entire contents of her desk into a crashing heap on the floor. She didn't flinch, just pressed the tip of her tongue into his ear instead. A groan that started in his groin ripped through him and he went over the edge completely. He turned and sat her on the desk, pressing her back flat as he moved hard between her legs. She kept her legs wrapped around his waist and they began to move together as he ravaged her neck and breasts with kisses, sucking, licking, and biting every inch of skin he could reach.

April squirmed under him, hating the zipper grinding into her, needing him now. Hard. Long. And thrusting. Deeply. "Jack. Jack." His name was a plea for release.

"Yes. Say it, April. What do you want?"

"You. Now." They were both panting heavily, the heat from their bodies making their skin slippery.

Jack yanked his wallet from his pocket and threw it down next to her head on the desk. Then he ripped his belt open, pushing his pants down, tugging them from under the legs at his waist. "Where? Where do you want me, April?" She squirmed as he spoke and he pulled her dress out from under her belt, unhooking her legs only long enough to slide it down her legs and fling it across the room.

He looked down at her and felt his knees begin to give. Bathed in white light, she wore only sheer yellow panties and the slim gold belt. As his gaze devoured her, her back arched, thrusting her breasts high in the air. "Where, April? For God's sake, where?"

Her hair was a wild mass splayed around her head as her gaze lowered from his eyes, moved down his chest, swept across his abdomen, and stopped when it encountered his throbbing erection. Without looking up, her voice thready with need, she answered, "Inside me, Jack. Deep inside me."

With a sound that was more growl than groan, Jack slipped the condom from his wallet and all but yanked it into place. He leaned over her, tamping down the incredible animalistic urge just to thrust into her. Instead he pushed his tongue into her mouth and slid his hand between her legs, pressing his finger inside of her. "This deep?" he asked against her lips. He pushed deeper. "Or this deep?"

April tightened her legs and pushed against him. "Deeper."

Jack's breath left him in a shuddering hiss, then he kissed her long and hard as his fingers slid out of her and he pressed himself against her instead. He pushed into her, slowly. The pain of restraint was excruciatingly thrilling and he knew then he could die from the pleasure of it. "Mine. You . . . are . . . mine."

He pushed himself completely into her and she met him thrust for thrust. Jack felt the last shred of civilized behavior slip away as his belly slapped against hers over and over. Giving and taking equally, he felt the need to possess her permanently—in this life, in their next life, and for all eternity.

Just at the brink he locked his gaze on hers, pausing for a fraction of a second. They said nothing, but in the next instant, as they both went over the edge, a look passed between them that bonded them, one to the other.

Irrevocably.

Jack pressed his full weight on her, shudders still racking his body. Only when April moaned softly did he pull himself together enough to shift his weight to his forearms, leaving his chest brushing against hers. He looked down at her face, but their position blocked most of the light. He wanted to see her eyes, wondering what she felt at that moment. Wondering if she felt like he did. Like the world had just spun into a new orbit.

She moaned again and he moved to get off of her, suddenly realizing how uncomfortable she must be. "Son of a bitch," he muttered as he pulled out of her and shifted away, angry at his total lack of consideration for her. His need for her had been so intense, so all-consuming . . . . He bit back another oath. He wanted her spinning in space with him, when the reality was she'd probably be happiest if he'd just get off of her.

"Don't leave me yet," she whispered, gripping his waist with her thighs to keep him close.

Feeling even more like a bastard, he immediately leaned back over and tucked his hands under her back and hips. "April, I'm so sorry."

She had started to grab on to his shoulders, anticipating his pulling her up, but his words stopped her and she tilted her face to him. "Why?"

How could one word contain so much wariness? "I'm handling this badly." He shook his head as if to clear it and pulled her upright. Her legs still wrapped around his waist, he turned and sat on the desk, then pulled her more deeply into his arms.

Pressing his lips against her hair, he whispered, "What just happened between us was incredible. I'm angry because I took you like a rutting bull on your desk, for God's sake." He lifted her chin so he could stare into her now-illuminated eyes. "At the very least, what we just shared deserved a soft bed and clean sheets."

April tightened her hold on him at the self-recrimination she saw in his eyes. If she ever doubted her ability to care deeply for someone again, that doubt was rapidly vanishing. He had to know she was an equal partner in what they'd just done, and where they'd done it. She searched for the words to tell him what she felt. Reaching up to caress his jaw, then his lips, she said simply, "If it bothers you, then next time make sure there's one around."

Jack looked confused, then surprised. Soon a wide smile spread across his face and he pressed a hard, fast kiss on her lips. He shifted her so she sat astride his lap and locked his gaze on hers. He was still smiling, but his tone was serious. "Lady, you scare the hell out of me."

April's smile faded a bit, but she couldn't keep the feelings that were flooding through her from showing in her eyes. "That makes two of us."

Jack's smile was tender, even a bit smug as he tucked a few stray curls behind her ears. "Well, what are we going to do about it?"

The cocoon aura they'd created with the suddenness and intensity of their lovemaking began to fade as reality reared its unwanted ugly head. "I don't know, Jack."

Hating the lost look that swept her features, he pressed a gentle kiss on the tip of her nose, then another one on her forehead. He tucked her against his chest and stared past her out the window. "I want to be with you. I don't think I can be here and not see you."

April stiffened briefly at the thought of seeing Jack around the resort and trying to respond to him as merely another guest. He was right. She could never settle for that now. So what did that mean? That they'd have an affair and then, when he went back to the States in a couple of weeks, say good-bye as if it had meant nothing?

The very idea was too painful to even contemplate and April forced herself to deal with the moment, not the future. Given her past, it was an almost impossible task not to try to protect herself. But she knew that if the alternative was ending their relationship now, she had no recourse but to go on. Pushing away all thoughts of their inevitable parting, she whispered against his chest, "I don't think I could let you."

Jack released the deep breath he'd been unaware of holding. Until she'd answered, he hadn't realized how devastated he'd have been if she'd gotten up and walked away. The simple truth was he wouldn't have let her, but he kept that to himself. He nuzzled her ear and said, "Then why don't we go and find that soft bed?"

April felt herself clench as hot shafts of desire shot through her at the idea of spending the rest of the night with Jack. Yet the idea of calmly putting on their clothes and strolling to his bungalow or hers made her feel oddly embarrassed. Which was totally ridiculous, given the fact she had just been writhing under him on her desk.

She hadn't a clue as to how to tell him this without sounding like a complete jackass or worse yet, hurting his feelings.

Thankfully, she was saved from the task when Jack leaned back slightly and said, "I, uh, I guess we have some cleaning up to do in here first though, huh?"

The sheepish look on his face was totally endearing, and she felt another piece of her heart slip away. She looked around at the havoc they'd wreaked and smiled. Partly in embarrassment, partly because it was just plain funny, she began to chuckle. Even in the semidarkness, she could make out the papers and file folders strewn across the floor, and she couldn't swear to it, but that looked like her dress hanging from the yucca tree in the corner of her office. Unable to stop, she began to laugh, hard.

Jack made his own quick assessment of the destruction and began to laugh, too. Between gasps for air, he said, "Would it help if I told you that I'd be willing to file folders for the next week if we could do this again right here, right now?"

Gasping half in laughter, half in desire, she had the urge to say "the hell with the filing" and press *him* back onto the desk. Instead she held on to him until their laughter faded, then quietly said, "I don't think that's what they had in mind when they named it a 'blotter.' "

Jack barked a laugh in surprise, hugged her tight, then stood up, holding her against him. "You have a wicked tongue, *mi tesoro*. Why don't we get dressed and clean up here, so we can go find out just how wicked it can be?"

Before she could respond, Jack leaned over and deposited her in her padded leather chair, then turned to begin rounding up their clothes. The awkward situation she'd feared was instead intimate, and she tucked her knees into the chair as she watched him stroll, unabashedly naked, around her office, slinging garments over his shoulder as he went.

Admiring the way the moonlight highlighted his sculpted backside and shoulders, April allowed herself to revel in the supremely sated feelings his lovemaking had inspired. There would be plenty of time for recriminations later, and she'd be damned if she wasn't going to stockpile some great memories to counterbalance them.

Jack strolled toward her and she found her gaze riveted between his legs. No doubt she'd have *plenty* of memories if the arousal he took no pains to hide from view was to be a normal part of their relationship.

"Arms up," he commanded, his tone smug.

She complied and he slid her dress over her head. He clearly enjoyed being looked at, and that excited her. The silky fabric caressed her newly resensitized skin and she had to refrain from reaching for his slowly swelling manhood.

Amazed at the strength of the instincts urging

her to go to him again, she quickly stood, fumbling with the buttons tangled under her hair, and looked around for her shoes. His low chuckle and the sound of a metal zipper being dragged upward reached her ears at the same time. Neither sound served to calm her tightened nerves.

In silent companionship Jack scooped up the mess on the floor and heaped it on the desk, while April attempted to at least sort it into stacks. There was no uneasiness; in fact, the way they worked together without having to speak kept the cocoon intact. April didn't dwell on the idea that Jack might fit into her life very easily if he wanted to. There was enough disappointment ahead, and building up hopes when she knew better would be painfully foolish.

Jack's sudden question made her aware of just how foolish it would be.

"What were you thinking about when I first came in tonight?"

April neatened the stack in front of her without really seeing it, easily recalling the moment. The conversation she'd had with Smithson at the wedding played quickly through her mind, again. Now was definitely not the time to discuss that part of her past. Nonetheless it served as a timely reminder of just what she'd be risking by getting involved with someone whose life was firmly rooted in the States.

Especially someone like Jack. She didn't know exactly what had sent him to the brink of burnout, but she'd bet it wasn't shooting weddings. Adopting a light smile, she tried for a glib response. "Would you be greatly disappointed if I said I was thinking about another man?" She'd meant it as a joke, a wry twist on the truth. She'd forgotten Jack's perceptive, miss-nothing gaze.

He rounded the desk slowly, resting his hip against the desk in a deceptively casual pose. "Who, April?" She started to turn away, but he caught her elbow in a gentle grip and tugged her back against him. "Who has you so tied up in knots that it took something as wild as what we have between us to unleash it?"

The undercurrent in his voice rocked her. If it had been jealousy she could have resorted to righteous indignation or wounded pride. Instead his tone had been one of fierce protectiveness, as if he wanted to know so he could run out and slay her dragons for her. She knew the idea was farfetched. She also knew she was right. And the temptation to let someone else fight her demons was so new, so overwhelming, she felt her knees begin to buckle under the strain of resisting the urge to give in to it.

Jack caught her against him and hugged her. Nothing could have prepared her for the effect that feeling his strong arms so firmly around her would create. There was nothing sexual in the embrace. It was gentle, protective, solid. She could no more resist his offer of help than pull away from his sheltering embrace. Ten long years of building that wall, brick by brick, and here it had all come crashing down in one thunderous roar. Clinging to him, she began to tremble.

"What is it, April? Tell me!"

"I'm afraid," she admitted, knowing he would take it wrong. He did.

"Of what? Who? My God, what have you been holding in all this time?"

She shook her head slowly, trying to sort out all the wild thoughts and images flying through her mind. Images of Smithson's casual announcement at the wedding clashed with flashbacks of Markham's face contorting in rage when she'd threatened to file charges. She saw again the lawyers pounding her with insulting, demeaning questions and the incessant flashbulbs blinding her every time she stepped outside. All the humiliation and degradation she'd been put through came back in such horrifying clarity, it was as if it had happened ten minutes ago, instead of ten years.

She clung to Jack, trying desperately to shove the whole thing from her mind, very much afraid that this time she wouldn't be able to—because he wouldn't let her. That was what frightened her. He wanted to help, but April sensed that if she told him the whole ugly story, she wouldn't have to worry about how their relationship would end.

Although she was clinging to him, Jack felt April struggle to pull herself together, and away from him. At least mentally. He'd never felt so ineffective in his life. He'd survived countless life-and-death situations. His ability to always remain clear and levelheaded no matter the crisis was partly what had won him so much recognition early on in his career. Locking his emotions away had been a struggle at first, but once he'd buried them, he'd never failed to get the job done, and it had eventually become a way of life.

Until now. The very idea that something was so horribly wrong in April's life that it could reduce the strong, independent woman he'd made wild love to a few minutes ago to a vulnerable, trembling mass of nerves terrified him. Terrified him to the point that he couldn't form a rational thought, much less come up with a sensible plan for calming her down and urging the story from her. And he'd built his entire career on his ability to do just that, for chrissakes!

Reacting purely on instinct, Jack swallowed his own fears and held on tightly, folding her completely in his arms. "It's okay, *mi tesoro*," he whispered against her hair. "It's okay. You don't have to tell me anything. But I swear I'll do whatever

I can to help you. I want to help you. Let me in, April. Please, trust me."

April continued to shake in his arms, and he wondered if she'd even heard him. Shoving aside every self-protective instinct he had, he vowed he would do anything, everything in his power to make her world right.

The realization that leaving her might have to be part of that solution made his eyes burn, and he viciously pushed the thought aside. If they had proven one thing tonight it was that between them, they had the power to obliterate her problems, at least for a while. And for now, that would have to be enough.

Jack pushed his hand under her hair and pulled her head back, bringing his lips down hard on hers, willing her to focus only on him. Her immediate response inflamed him and he kept on kissing her until he was certain she was responding to him and him alone. Only when he was certain her ghosts were no longer between them did he relax his grip and gentle his kisses.

Instead of pulling away, she began to push him back on the desk, and he let out a deep groan as her body rubbed against his. She kissed his face, his neck, and the bare chest exposed through his unbuttoned shirt. Her tongue and lips pulled at his nipples and he gripped her hips, pulling her down hard against him.

When she spoke, he went right over the edge. "Jack, make love to me again. I need you."

Without a second thought, he pulled her up into his arms, turned and sent the entire contents of her desk back to the floor, then proceeded to do just as she'd asked.

SEVEN

April had successfully managed to stay away from her office all morning, but Carmen's urgent note made it impossible to avoid any longer. Crossing the compound to the side entrance, April glanced around at the expanse of lawn, which was empty but for a few guests. It was hard to believe the wedding had taken place here less than a week ago. Her mind automatically turned to Jack.

She couldn't repress the smile that touched her lips as she let herself into the cool interior of the lobby. If anyone had told her a week ago she'd become involved in a torrid relationship with one of her guests in such a short time, she'd have checked that person into the Cove's infirmary for sunstroke. Yet, it was true.

She ducked into the stairwell, deciding to catch the elevator on the second floor. With her body flaming in remembrance of last night, she needed privacy for a few moments. She raced up the stairs, hoping Carmen wouldn't follow her into her office. She had a feeling her expression when she laid her eyes on her desk for the first time would be a dead giveaway. And while Carmen was the closest friend she'd had since coming to Mexico, April knew she wasn't deaf to the resort grapevine. She needed time to get used to her relationship with Jack and wasn't up to discussing it with anyone, not even Carmen.

She reached the second-floor landing, remembering the way the previous evening had ended. She'd expected to feel awkward, but Jack had made her laugh as he belatedly offered her the midnight snack of cheese, hard rolls, and carafe of wine he'd brought in the cooler. They'd picnicked on her desk before straightening it yet again, then he'd tucked her hand in his and walked her back to her bungalow in companionable silence. Even their parting hadn't been difficult; he'd merely kissed her at the door and left.

That "simple" kiss flashed back through her mind in stunning detail. She decided maybe she'd use the stairs all the way to the top floor.

Upon reaching her office, she took a deep breath and plastered a smile on her face before pushing open the door. As expected, Carmen was waiting for her. "Hi," April said, her voice overly bright. "What was so urgent that I had to drop everything and come running?" When Carmen didn't return her smile, April's began to fade. "Okay, let me have it."

"We got a letter from an Oaxacan state official stating that several complaints have reached them regarding your hiring practices. They've scheduled a special hearing and they urge you to attend."

"What?" April quickly switched mental gears. She knew her practice of hiring the local Indians, mostly Zapotecs, had come under fire from some of the local Mexican bureaucrats, but she was stunned that they'd taken their complaints to the state government. "When is the hearing?"

Carmen looked morose. "That's just it. It's tomorrow."

"I can't possibly get to Oaxaca by tomorrow!"

"I know. I've already tried to get you on a flight out of Santa Cruz but Aerovias Qaxaqueñas is booked. The letter was mailed over a—"

"Don't tell me, I'm very familiar with the local postal service here. If people in the U.S. only knew how good they have it." With a disgusted sigh, April dropped into the chair across from Carmen's desk. Not for the first time, she wished she'd invested in a helicopter along with the helipad. As it was, the helipad was just a perk for guests who chose that mode of transportation. "Shoot! You know what's going to happen if I don't show."

"Show up where?"

The question came from behind her, and the familiar deep voice made her spin in her seat. "Jack!" It was amazing, given her current problems, what the mere sound of his voice did to her nervous system. Of course, the fact that he had on faded black gym shorts and an unbuttoned print shirt which parted to show a healthy expanse of tanned chest may have played a small part in her sudden lapse of memory.

She had to stop for a split second to remember what it was he'd asked. "Hi. I'm supposed to be in Oaxaca by this time tomorrow, and unless I want to risk life and limb driving there, I'm out of luck."

Jack let his hands drop from the door frame overhead and came into the office. April scooted back in her chair as he perched on the side of Carmen's desk, forcing her gaze away from his thighs and her thoughts away from how intimately she'd touched them last night. It would have been easier if she'd missed Carmen's appreciative stare and the quick wink her secretary had sent in her direction when Jack wasn't looking. Unfortunately, she hadn't. Apparently the grapevine worked even better than she thought.

Any last-ditch effort at regaining her equilibrium was shot to pieces when Jack grinned and nodded his head toward her office door. "I think I have a solution to your problem. Why don't we let Carmen get back to work, and go into your office to work out the details." He didn't phrase it as a question, he simply turned to Carmen and said, "Does that letter in your hand have something to do with this?"

Carmen nodded silently and Jack reached over and slipped it from her fingers. He folded it in half and handed it to April unread, then stood. "We'll take care of this mess." Then he shot Carmen one of his heartbreaker grins and added, "Could you handle any major crises that crop up in the next few minutes?"

Carmen melted like ice left under the hot Mexican sun. "*Sí, Señor* Jack. No problem."

Jack sauntered around the desk into her office, but it took a gentle kick on the shin from Carmen to jerk April out of her stunned disbelief. How dare he stroll in here and order her secretary around! Conveniently forgetting he'd offered her a solution to a very big problem, April shot out of her chair. She aimed a glare at Carmen, knowing it wouldn't do any good. She wasn't exactly immune to Jack's smiles either. That just increased her anger, and she stormed into her office.

Resisting the urge to slam the door, she closed it with a forceful click. April didn't attempt to get control of herself; instead, she silently thanked Jack for making her reentry into the room they'd so thoroughly used the night before easier than she'd dared to hope.

He was sitting in one of the chairs nearest to the door and she stalked over to him, glad to have the height advantage for a change. Planting her hands on her hips, she let him have it with both barrels. "Who the hell do you think you are? Just because we—" She faltered a bit as his benign smile turned wicked and knowing.

"Because we what, *mi tesoro*?"

"Don't call me that!" Knowing she sounded like a shrew, especially since he knew just how much she liked it when he called her his "treasure," she tempered her voice. In a cooler, albeit clipped tone, she said, "While I appreciate your offer to help me, I wish you'd stop interfering in my work. Especially between me and my staff. It's taken me ten years to build up my reputation and I'll be damned—"

"Hey, slow down." His smile faded to a look of real concern. He stood and reached for her, but let his hands drop when she stepped back. "I didn't mean to usurp your authority. Now or yesterday. Besides, your employees respect the hell out of you. You've more than earned it and I doubt I could change that, even if I wanted to. Which I don't, by the way."

April felt the fight drain out of her. On a more conciliatory note, she tried to make her point. "I know. But you have to understand how hard it is as a woman to command respect in this country. And no matter what I've done or for how long, you'd be amazed how naturally the people here will turn to a male voice of authority. I'm sorry I overreacted. I know you're only trying to help."

Jack absorbed her quiet statements, realizing anew just how much she'd struggled to make a life for herself here. And based on last night, he knew her troubles had begun long before she'd come to Mexico. His desire to know her, all about her, intensified tenfold.

A slow grin split his features as he recalled her current predicament. Maybe he had a solution to both of their problems. "At the risk of being gut-punched, why don't you let me take you away from all this for a while?"

April had to smile when he took a step back and covered his abdomen in a mock feint. "Don't I wish," she responded honestly. The effect his size and power had on her was always present, but now that her anger had abated, the awareness turned sexual again and she found herself wanting to touch him.

"Your wish is my command. You clear your schedule and I can get you to Oaxaca by late this afternoon."

It took a second or two for his words to sink in. When they did her eyes widened in disbelief. "And how do you propose to do that? Fly me there in your private jet?"

"Something like that," he answered, sounding suspiciously serious. "Now stop wasting time. Go play CEO and delegate, then pack your bags and meet me in the lobby by noon." Purposely misreading her raised eyebrows, he added, "It'll take us an hour just to get to that potholed strip of pavement that Santa Cruz tries to pass off as an airport."

Despite her recent lecture on his controlling habits, April laughed. She thought about telling him that all the flights were booked, but knew it would have been a waste of breath. "Has anyone told you you're absolutely incorrigible?"

A wry grin formed on his lips. "Once or twice. Do we have a deal?"

Knowing this was a fight she wouldn't win, she gave in gracefully. "Only because I have to attend this meeting, yes. Are you going to tell me the details?"

"Trust me." He walked over to her office door.

"I didn't think so," she muttered. April stared at her desk, trying to compile a quick list of what needed to be done before she left, but recalling last night instead.

"Of course, if you keep staring at that desk like that, we won't be leaving this room till dinner."

April's head shot up and their eyes locked. "I wasn't even . . ." She let the sentence die as she realized it would have been a lie. "Is that why you came up here in the first place?"

Jack walked slowly back to the desk. The layers of protection she'd built hadn't been completely torn down and her instincts urged her to move, to put distance between them. His unwavering gaze rooted her to the spot.

"Honestly?" he queried, a faint smile ghosting his lips.

She tried to gulp, couldn't, and settled for a nod. She could only describe his expression as . . . predatory.

From across the desk, he said, "I have to admit to wanting to see you in this room all professional and businesslike." He braced his hands on the desk and leaned toward her. "And I won't deny that I wondered if I could get you to take that stick out of your hair and let it fall to your shoulders. I liked it all loose and sexy."

He pushed off her desk and walked slowly around to stand in front of her. His voice was a deep, throaty whisper. "And I'd be lying if I told you I hadn't spent the better part of today fantasizing about taking you here again, only this time in bright sunlight."

April drew in a deep breath and held it there, praying he wouldn't touch her, knowing she'd hate him if he didn't. "And now?" she asked, her voice tight.

He moved closer, until his partially bared chest almost, but not quite, brushed against the front of her cotton blouse. "And now that I know I'll have you almost all to myself for the next couple of days, I'll settle for this." He slid the ivory stick out of her hair, then in one fluid motion tucked one hand beneath the heavy mass on her neck, placed the other on the small of her back, and pulled her against him.

Stopping for one long heartbeat, he simply stared into her eyes; then his drifted shut as he pressed a slow, probing kiss against her parted lips.

Only a dead woman wouldn't have responded. And she was far from dead. Small, urgent sounds formed in her throat and she leaned into him, not caring about the unlocked door or that his hands had strayed to the front of her blouse. She pushed his open shirt back to his shoulders and ran her hands over his chest, reveling in the compact hardness of each muscle.

On a deep groan, Jack slowly pulled his mouth from hers and covered her hands with his own. Twining his fingers with hers, an action that shocked April because it somehow felt even more intimate than the caresses they'd just shared, he let their joined hands fall to their sides. She looked up at him and he leaned down so his forehead rested on hers. She could feel the movement of his bare abdomen against her rib cage with each shuddering breath he took.

"You just let me *think* I'm in control here, don't you?"

Confused, April asked, "What? You think *I* am?"

"What I think is that I could very easily get lost in you."

Every muscle in April's body tightened in response to his quiet statement, whether in fear or desire she wasn't sure. It was probably a little of both. But regardless of the reason, she knew she couldn't walk away from whatever he was offering her. It was only a little reassuring to know that just maybe they were both well and truly caught in the web. "I'm . . . I need to get some work done if I'm—we're—going to Oaxaca."

Jack's smile was as sudden as it was wicked, and her heart pounded in response. "Can you get it done by noon?"

"Only if you leave my office this second."

"You drive a hard bargain, sweetheart." He dropped a quick kiss on the tip of her nose, paused for a split second, his lips hovering over hers, and let her go. He walked to the door, then turned back. "Speaking of driving: Do you have a resort vehicle that the Cove can spare for a few days?"

Her expression suddenly wary, she asked, "Sure, but you aren't thinking we can drive there. The roads over the mountains are unreliable at best, treacherous at worst."

"Actually, if we had the time, that might be fun." He raised his eyebrows in a mocking imitation of her response. "But since we don't, I figured I'd just fly you there in my plane. We'll need to leave the car at the airport for the drive back." At her further look of amazement, he added, "What, you didn't think I pushed that Jeep all the way from L.A., did you?" Not waiting for a response, he winked, opened the door, and left.

It took a few seconds for her to snap her mouth shut. When she did, her lips formed a smile as with a renewed sense of purpose she hurried to clear her desk.

The ride to Santa Cruz airport was long, dusty, and bumpy, but at least the engine didn't conk out. The pickup truck wasn't much better than the Jeep he'd pushed into the resort, but April hadn't wanted to put one of the resort's vans out of service for the few days they'd be away and Jack had dismissed the idea of a taxi. So she had arranged for them to use one of the Cove's work trucks. Her backside was sore, though.

She had a sudden image of Jack pushing the Jeep over the badly rutted roads, and cringed. Now that she knew that on top of it all he'd flown here from L.A., his fatigue the day they met was even more understandable. She was amazed he'd made it to the bungalow on his own two feet.

He pulled into a space behind the main building that served as terminal, flight gate, and air control tower and got her first look at Jack's plane. "It's very . . . small." She'd meant to say "nice," but the truth had snuck out instead.

"Great, isn't she? Cessna 172, seats four, flies like a dream, and as of six months ago, she's all mine." He hopped out, then turned to get their bags from the backseat. "Just let me stow these on board," he called to her. "I have to do a preflight check and run my flight plans past whoever's playing controller today."

April nodded and watched him in stunned silence as he efficiently went about the preparations. His quick, deft movements as he looked over the plane reassured her. She was still getting used to the idea that he was a pilot. The long ride to the airport had been loud and not real conducive to conversation. She'd spent the first half of the trip trying to figure out where "pilot" fit in with "photographer" and the second half determining to have the answer by the time they returned to the Cove.

She hopped down from the truck and, after making sure he hadn't forgotten anything, locked it up. Jack had gone inside the rather rustic terminal, so she wandered over to the plane.

"We're all set," he said, coming up behind her just minutes later. "Your chariot awaits."

A few minutes later she was strapped into the copilot's seat and watched the tiny airport disappear from view as Jack banked the plane and headed toward the mountains to the east.

"How long have you been flying?" She had to raise her voice to be heard even though the cockpit was barely big enough for the two of them.

Jack dropped his headphones around his neck and smiled as he answered. "Let's see, I'm thirty-five, so, I guess about ten years or so. My uncle flew and I was always interested. Later on I realized it was a skill that would come in handy with my career, so I got my license."

He made it sound as if he'd learned to drive a car so he could get to work. Yelling questions in a noisy plane wasn't the best way to learn about his past, but she was too curious to wait for a better opportunity. "Just what type of career do you have? I thought you were a photographer."

He looked over at her, his translucent green eyes probing hers for several long seconds before he turned his attention back to flying. Just when she thought he wasn't going to answer, he spoke.

"I'm actually a photojournalist." Jack cast a quick glance at her, then looked back at the panel in front of him. Since she absorbed that bit of news in silence, he went on. "Some of the places I go for stories aren't exactly conveniently located off a highway exit. Flying planes and occasionally helicopters has gotten me into places I couldn't have reached otherwise." He didn't add that it had also gotten him out of those places in one piece a few times too, but another quick glance at April's face told him it wasn't necessary.

It should have unsettled him that she read him so well, but instead it was strangely reassuring. Still, he wished he knew what she was thinking. He'd hoped to know a bit more about her background before revealing more of his—at least what it was that had spooked her and sent her running from the United States all the way to the other end of Mexico. He didn't like not knowing if something he'd done in his past might somehow turn her against him. But he wouldn't lie to her. She deserved to know as much about him as he did about her.

"So, you worked mostly foreign assignments?"

He sensed there was more to that question than random interest, but he answered it honestly. "Yes," he responded, raising his voice over the noise of the unpressurized cabin. "Mostly the Middle East, occasionally Europe or South America. Usually political or governmental-unrest kind of stuff."

April blew out a deep breath. She knew that kind of "stuff," as he called it, could be dangerous, that he could have been killed. The very idea of him risking his life repeatedly to get a few pictures and a story turned her stomach into a lead ball.

All at once things started to fall into place, little fragments of conversation she'd had with him regarding his reasons for being at the Cove. "Do you think you'll go out on another assignment when you get back to L.A.?"

Jack jerked his gaze toward her and held it as long as he thought he could. How in the hell was he supposed to answer such a loaded question at twelve thousand feet? "I don't know, April." It was a far more truthful response than he'd thought it would be. It was also the only one he had.

April lapsed into her own thoughts and Jack turned his attention back to flying the plane. It was killing him not to ask her what she was thinking: about him, his career, his future plans. About whether she would like to be a part of the latter. He realized that it was the sudden importance of his need to know that kept him silent.

They were lucky to encounter little disturbance over the mountains, or air pockets as they crossed over the dense tropical forests near the city of Oaxaca, but April still sighed a breath of relief once they were safely on the ground. As he'd promised, it was mid-afternoon when they deplaned. She stood with their gear as Jack disappeared into the Oaxaca terminal to find the *transporte terrestre* counter to arrange for one of the yellow *taxis* to take them the nine or so kilometers into the city.

She hadn't been to the ancient city in several years. The state capital, it also had the largest population of the native Zapotecs. An intensely proud and private group, they were regarded by many as below second class, mainly due to their lack of education. A wry grimace crossed her face as she railed inwardly at the harsh irony that it was this attitude that kept them from being educated in the first place. She thought about the meeting tomorrow and felt a wave of fatigue at the task ahead of her.

She suddenly wished she were just here with Jack to rest and relax. It was disturbing to realize just how much she needed that break. At least this time away from the pressures of the Cove might help her figure out where she was headed with Jack. She turned her thoughts to the night ahead and shivered, as if the breeze that whipped across the open concourse was chilly rather than muggy and warm.

The idea of spending an entire night in a soft bed surrounded by Jack's big, hard body made her skin heat again. She jumped when a large hand gripped her shoulder.

"Sorry. You looked a million miles away. What were you thinking about?" Jack put his arm around her shoulders and herded her toward the taxi that was waiting about fifty feet away.

The flush on her skin deepened. She knew it

was silly of her, but she couldn't come out and say she'd been picturing them in bed making love with wild abandon. "Just about the trip. I guess we should be getting to the hotel. Carmen made reservations at the El Presidente; it's one of the nicest hotels in Oaxaca."

He leaned down to whisper in her ear. "Does it have big beds and clean sheets?"

She smiled up at him. Had he guessed her thoughts? "I should hope so. Why?"

"If it has that and room service, I don't care if it's a Motel 6."

She laughed and watched the cabbie watching Jack load their luggage into the trunk. If a tourist showed the slightest inclination to help himself, most locals were more than happy to indulge them. Their driver was apparently no exception. "I wouldn't count on room service if you need sustenance quickly."

Jack's smile turned wicked as they climbed into the backseat. She moved to the far side to allow him some room in the cramped quarters, but he pulled her tight to his side. "If you're in the room with me, I promise, I'll never starve."

Out of the corner of her eye April noticed the taxi driver watching them in the rearview mirror. She shifted a micrometer away from Jack—all his grip would allow—and said, "*Hotel El Presidente, 5 de Mayo 300, por favor.*"

She gave the instructions in her haughtiest CEO voice, but the effect was ruined when, in perfect Spanish, Jack added, "And there's extra in it for you if you get us there pronto. *Comprendes*?"

Apparently the cabbie did, because he turned his attention back to the road and floored the gas pedal. April would have been flung against the door as they careened out of the lot if not for Jack's hold on her. "You might want to tell Mario Junior up there to slow down if you want us to get there in one piece," she muttered, only half upset that Jack had taken over—again.

"April?"

"What?" she grumped, not trusting his soft voice.

"Be quiet and kiss me. We'll be there before I let you up for air."

As usual, he was right. But she didn't mind so much this time.

The *El Presidente* was actually a converted sixteenth-century convent, a fact that amused Jack to no end. His amusement faded, however, when he found that Carmen had booked them into adjoining rooms. Jack immediately asked for different accommodations, but this time April overruled him.

He glared at her as she accepted the room keys, but kept silent until they were in their rooms. The only smile she got out of him was when she'd quickly stepped in and prevented the bellman from taking Jack's silver camera case. Now that they were all alone, she wished she could think of something else that would make him smile again.

Jack leaned back against the closed door, eyeing her as she stood in front of the window across the room. "Did I miss something?"

She didn't pretend not to understand. "No."

He pushed off the door and closed the short distance between them. "Then why the two rooms?"

April shrugged but didn't look away. "This is all still new to me, and I just thought it might be best if we had some space. I don't know, just in case." As her voice trailed off, she thought she saw the anger leave his expression and his eyes darken in concern.

"In case I learn something in the next two days that would make me want my own room?" She looked away, and he reached out and pulled her to him by her upper arms. "Look at me."

She realized she must have mistaken the look of concern. His voice contained barely concealed fury. She looked up at him and it was confirmed by the icy paleness of his green eyes.

"I want to know you, April. I intend to know you. Better than anyone else, more thoroughly than anyone ever will. If that idea scares you then join the crowd—it scares me too. But I'm not hiding, and I'm not running. The woman who kissed me under that tree wouldn't either. That's the woman I want."

Shaking with need and in fear of the wild emotions his heated statements had set off in her, she tried to pull out of his grasp. He wouldn't let her go. "If you want to know me then you're going to have to take all of me, Jack Tango. The woman who made love to you on her own desk is a very new part of me." She didn't have to add that it was a part only Jack had ever known; the flare of his pupils told her he understood that. "But I'm not into playing games either. I just know that there are parts of me, of my life, that may make you change your mind, okay? You ask me to trust you, and I want to. You want to talk scared? You don't even know the half of it."

Anything else she was about to say was cut off as his mouth came down hard on hers. He kissed her as if his life depended on it, as if her life depended on it. She kissed him back because she was very afraid that one day it *might*, and that she couldn't count on him being there then. He was here now, and that had to be enough.

Jack moved from her lips to her throat; he pulled her arms around his neck and moved his hands down her sides to her hips. The fear in her voice when she'd lashed back at him had been expected, and still he'd felt an overwhelming urge to carry her to the bed and push deep inside of her until she never doubted him again.

It was the certainty in her voice, however, that caused a cold finger of dread to creep into his heart. What if she didn't let him help her? And, God help him, what would he do if she asked him to and he didn't know how?

He yanked his lips from her shoulder and forced himself to gentle his grip. He pulled back and waited until she looked up at him. Her eyes were huge and such a deep shade of brown, he thought he might drown. He felt his heart drop to his stomach at the trace of resignation he saw in them. "Tell me, April," he commanded, his voice made harsh out of fear. "It's the only way I can prove to you I won't run. And I don't think this relationship can go any farther until you know that."

Her bottom lip, reddened from his kisses, trembled slightly, and he damned himself for putting her through this.

"Okay. But not this minute. I need—"

Her voice broke off in a strangled cry and Jack pressed a gentle kiss to her lips, then pulled her head to his chest. Wrapping his arms more tightly around her, he whispered, "Yeah, it's okay. I know."

He dropped soft kisses on her hair and stared out the window behind her into the waning Mexican sunshine. "Listen, why don't I get out of here for a while. I'm sure you have some heavy-duty planning to do for the meeting and I'd like to explore the area and set up a few shots for tomorrow."

After a pause she said, "All right."

Her voice was rough with unshed tears, and it took all his will to let her go. He scooped up his canvas bag and quickly loaded it with the few things he'd need for his scouting trip. "I'll probably be out till dark. If you want, I can have them send up something for you to eat." He chanced a look at her. She'd turned her gaze out the window. "Or we can have a late meal out somewhere. I'll find a place while I'm out."

His easy manner cost him a great deal, but it was worth it when he saw the tension in her shoulders lessen as she relaxed slightly. "Sounds good. If I get hungry before then I'll call for something." Her voice was softer, but she kept her back to him.

With nothing else to say, Jack walked to the door.

"Jack?"

Her voice stopped him and he turned to find her facing him. "Yeah?"

"Thank you."

The words wobbled, but her face was a mask of strength. In that moment Jack admitted to himself that he loved her. "We will talk when I get back."

"Yes."

"And I'm canceling the other room. We will

share the same bed." He left the room, his hold on his control not strong enough to wait for a response. He almost fell to his knees when her whispered response reached his ears anyway.

"I hope so."

EIGHT

April crumpled the sheet of paper containing her tenth try at a coherent speech for the meeting tomorrow and aimed it at the small wicker basket she'd moved closer to the coffee table. She couldn't get Jack's parting words out of her head. She jumped at every sound outside the door and her gaze kept straying to the clock on the table by the wall.

Where was he?

She pushed herself off the low couch and paced the length of the room, massaging her lower back as she went. She peered out the window to the street one story below. It wasn't dark yet, but it was getting close.

April fought down the frustration that had been

steadily increasing since Jack had taken off. Deep down she knew he'd been trying to help, to give her the space she'd asked for. But the minute the door had closed behind him she'd wanted to run after him and beg him to listen. Sitting here for several hours had only provided her with too much time to go over in infinite detail all the horrible events she thought she'd blocked from her mind forever.

Senator Smithson's off-the-cuff comments about Markham possibly tossing his hat in the presidential ring had been bad enough; having to deal with Jack's all-too-perceptive gaze on top of it had made repressing her past again impossible.

She paced over to the small refrigerator and pulled out a bottle of mango juice. The tangy flavor only served to remind her taste buds of the fact that she hadn't eaten since the light snack Jack had brought along on the drive to Santa Cruz. Lord, that seemed like days ago, instead of hours.

She plopped down on the couch again and pulled a throw pillow onto her lap, fiercely concentrating on untangling the gaily colored tassels that adorned the corners and avoiding the clock, the window, and the door. Maybe Jack had left her alone for the precise reason that he'd known she'd rehash her past over and over, so that by the time he came back she'd be dying to get it off her chest. As farfetched as this sounded, she sensed it was the truth. It irritated her further to admit that, if that was his plan, it had worked.

"Dammit, Tango! Where are you?" As if her words had summoned him, the door to the room swung inward and he ducked his imposing frame inside.

"Miss me?" Jack poured his heart and soul into a charming smile, hoping she wouldn't notice the questions he couldn't keep out of his eyes.

"Yes," she answered simply.

If that one quietly spoken word hadn't been enough of a clue to her inner thoughts, the pile of crumpled notes in the wastebasket and the fact that she was all but twisting the fringe off the pillow clutched in her lap erased any doubt. He forced himself to cross over to the small desk and relieve himself of his gear before going to her.

He'd made it back across the room but came to a stop on the opposite side of the coffee table, unsure of how, or where, to start. Frustrated by his uncustomary loss for the right words, he jammed his hands into the pockets of his shorts and waited for her to say something, praying it would help to guide him. Dammit, he shouldn't have left her alone!

"Are you thirsty? There's some juice in the fridge."

It wasn't exactly the information he'd been looking for, but it told him enough. "No. I found a cafe in the *zócalo* that looked good. You want to go out for a while?" Before we talk? This last question might as well have been said out loud, for he knew she had heard it as plainly as he had.

"Not unless . . ." She put the pillow beside her in a very specific manner, as if it were a shield being lowered. She looked back up at him, her expression closed, but steady. "No, I don't. I think we should talk first."

"Okay. I don't think they take reservations anyway." His attempt to lighten the mood failed and his smile slid from his face. "Where do you want me to sit?"

The question seemed to take her by surprise; then she answered, "I think, maybe, next to me. Is that all right?"

It was a tiny crack in her composure, but a telling one, and Jack felt his heart begin to pound. "That's better than all right." The words came out deeper, a bit rougher, than he'd intended, but he didn't care. He sat on the couch next to her, close enough to touch her if he wanted to. Or if she needed him to.

"Do you want to ask me questions? Or—"

"I want to know what happened, April. What made you leave the U.S. ten years ago?"

"I want to tell you, need to tell you. But I have a question first: Why is this so important to you?"

Jack immediately understood what had prompted the question and damned himself for feeling hurt and angry that she doubted him. Apparently she had good reason to, so he tamped his feelings down and answered her as honestly as he could. "This is not Jack the journalist wanting to know your sordid past."

His muscles clenched when he saw her flinch at his unwitting choice of words. He had to ball his hands into fists to keep from dragging her into his arms and kissing her, making love to her until no trace of doubt was left as to his motives. He swallowed hard. "I'm sorry, that was unintentional."

He focused his gaze on hers, willing her not to look away as he continued. She didn't. "And that's part of why I have to know. Something has hurt you—hurt you so deeply that you've forced yourself to diminish beautiful, natural qualities in you in order to protect yourself. Until now. I've seen them, April. I want them. I want you to want them. Until I understand how the two parts of you mesh, and why they exist in the first place, I can't be sure that I won't say or do something indirectly that will hurt you."

His voice had dropped further, becoming very intense as he willed her to believe him, trust him—knowing with a fear he'd never felt that she could, but might choose not to, and that there wasn't a damn thing he could do about it. "I don't want to hurt you, *mi tesoro*. I want to help heal you."

Her eyes became glassy but her gaze never wavered. "Okay."

He watched her hands unclench and thought she would reach for his, had purposely put them on his knees within easy reach. But she turned to look at the wall and the door to the hallway. Digging his fingers into his kneecaps, he waited in silence for her to start.

"Back in the States, I used to work for a large hotel chain. My father had various business dealings with the chain owner and after I'd gotten my degree in hotel management, he arranged for an interview for me. I, uh, started as a reservation clerk and worked my way steadily into management."

Jack noticed she hadn't named names and wondered who she was protecting. Still, he remained silent, experience telling him that it would all come out if he could just be patient. It was the hardest assignment he'd ever given himself.

"I'd been working for . . . the hotel, for about five years when . . ." Her voice faded away and her gaze shifted to her hands.

"It's okay, April. Take your time." He watched her draw in her breath and straighten her spine somewhat and had to stifle the gentle urge to grin. Whatever had happened, her pride had survived the battle. He ignored the clutch near his heart.

"My boss made advances toward me and I turned him down." It all came out in one unbroken rush.

She darted a quick glance at him but hurried on as if she knew she'd be able to get through this only once and didn't dare give him the chance to stop her. "This went on for a while. Each time it . . . each time I politely declined he became uglier. I really thought he'd move on to someone else."

She ducked her head for a moment and rubbed her hand over her face. When she continued, her voice was softer, but laced with a thread of steel that was like ice piercing cotton. "Unfortunately, he did. I found a coworker of mine in the bathroom while on break one day. She, uh, she was in tears, almost hysterical."

April took a deep breath and faced him. Her skin was white, her eyes were hollow. "He'd raped her. In his office, he'd pulled her down and—" Her voice died on a choked sob.

Jack tried to pull her against him but she pushed him away with a hard shove. When she continued her eyes were hard and furious. "I urged her to come forward, told her what had happened to me and that together we could nail him. But she wouldn't do it. She was afraid to shame her family and she said she needed the job."

"What did you do?"

She went on as if she hadn't heard him, but Jack wasn't offended. He knew the look of cold fury in her eyes wasn't directed at him but at the son of a bitch she'd worked for.

"I told my father—something I should have done earlier, but I thought I could handle it myself. He was my dad's friend and I guess I didn't want to hurt my father by telling him. In retrospect I guess I was also ashamed, like it was my fault somehow."

Jack's grunt told her what he thought of that theory, and she looked at him, really looked at him, for the first time in the past several minutes.

"You have to understand that my father comes from the old school. Oh, he has respect for women—as long as they stay in their positions. My mother had died when I was a teenager and he held her up as a constant example to me. My mom was also from the old school that said a woman's sole function was to cater to her husband, family, and home—in that order. As you can imagine, we argued frequently." She allowed herself a small smile at that, but it quickly faded. "So you can see why I kept quiet. But after what happened to Frannie I just couldn't. I felt like it was my fault because I hadn't told someone sooner."

"What did your father do?"

"Well, he . . . he . . ." She looked away briefly, blinking at the moisture that coated her eyes. Looking back at Jack, her tone strong if somewhat wavery, she said, "He didn't believe me. He said I was mistaking a family friendship for something dirty. He blamed my insistence on living on campus while I was at college. According to him, campus life had put my mind in the gutter and nice girls didn't talk like that."

"Did you tell him about your coworker?" Jack's heart was pounding and he had an intense desire to go out and beat the living daylights out of someone. He had gone right past impartial listener to primal human with a need to avenge his own.

"No. There was no point, Jack," she added when he started to speak. "The subject was closed and he forbid me to speak of it again. But I couldn't let it go. Not and live with myself."

"You filed charges? Alone?"

The proud defiance in her shoulders was ruined by the hard cynicism in her eyes. "Oh yeah. I sure did."

"Don't tell me any more."

Stunned by his fervent plea, it took a second before her entire posture changed. She started to bolt but Jack reached for her, grabbing her arm with just enough force to make sure she didn't escape. "Don't. Don't you dare think I don't want to hear because I'm ashamed." He moved her chin with his other hand, all but dragging her gaze up to meet his. She was furious. Good. So was he.

"I've seen things, heard things, that would sicken you beyond all imagination. I don't scare off easily, April." Gentling his grip when a trace of fear crept into her eyes, he pulled her against him and held her as tightly as he thought she'd let him, knowing he'd never be close enough until he was buried inside of her again.

He nudged her forehead with his nose, feeling exalted that she was holding him every bit as tightly, and whispered, "Sweetheart, I'm a journalist."

She stiffened convulsively. He wasn't surprised, so he waited for her to relax, knowing this part of it had to be dealt with now. Letting out a sigh of relief when her shoulders curved toward him again, he went on. "And because of that, I, better than most, have a pretty accurate idea of what happened to you. They made you out to be the worst kind of slut and dragged your reputation, and your family's along with it, through the slime. And I don't guess dear old dad was much help." His tone was full of contempt and disgust. When she'd needed him most, the man in her life had deserted her.

"No. His reputation in the business community was very precious to him and since he'd written me off, he moved quickly to preserve what he had left."

"I'm so sorry, sweetheart. So I guess the bastard got off and you came down here to spend time with your grandfather." He set her back a few inches, his hands on her shoulders, needing her to look at him when he spoke. "Do you have any idea how much I respect you? Not only what you did then, but for what you've accomplished here?"

She didn't answer, but her eyes filled with tears.

"Damn him to hell! Damn them both to hell!" Jack's fingers tightened on her shoulders. "If it means anything to you, I want you to know that your response to me, the way you make me feel—"

"Don't."

Jack stopped, stunned—and more than a bit hurt.

"Don't what? Don't tell you that I—"

"No! There's more, Jack."

"Unless you want to relive it, I'm not about to make you go through the whole damn trial. I already feel like hell for making you go through as much as you have."

She just shook her head slowly, a look of remorse and pain crossing her face. "That's not it. I, you . . . you should know who . . . It was Alan Markham."

"*Who* was Ala—Holy hell! *Senator* Alan Markham was the man who molested you?" Jack got up off the couch, shock and head-pounding fury splitting his attention equally.

"Yes. Only he wasn't a senator then; he had only announced his intentions." She rose from the couch and stood before the window. "My father was a major backer of his campaign."

Jack swung around as all the pieces fell together in a sickening lurch. "Then the campaign to impugn you must have been a humdinger if it was politically backed. Wait a minute, your father didn't help him finance the smear—"

April turned around. "No. But I'm not too sure it wasn't because he didn't want to. I imagine there might have been a sticky conflict of interest." It was crystal clear to Jack that April felt he had wanted to.

"Why don't I remember the case?"

"Ten years is a long time. Maybe you were out of the country on assignment."

"Maybe." Something niggled at the back of Jack's mind. "Wait a minute. I might have been out of the country, but Franklin wasn't. But the name Morgan doesn't—"

"How about de la Torre?"

Jack's head whipped up as the name clicked. "But you—"

"Are April Marie de la Torre. My mother's maiden name is Morgan. When I moved here it just seemed easier. Besides, I didn't want Gramps to be hurt if the press tracked me down."

"He wouldn't have cared."

Her unfocused gaze sharpened immediately. "How do you know that?"

Jack felt like he'd been sucker-punched. She still didn't completely trust him. "Because the few times you've talked about him your face got all dreamy and innocent." He arched his eyebrow in an imitation of hers. "Yeah, it does, April. That part of you didn't die completely, and I suspect your grandfather had something to do with that."

Her expression faltered, and he took two steps toward her before forcing himself to stop. "Come here." He didn't hold his arms out; some remnant of self-protection or a need to test her feelings kept him from doing it. He didn't bother to examine the reasons. He just knew in his gut that she had to come to him.

"What if I do?"

He felt a burning behind his eyes at her last ditch-effort to save herself in case she'd misread him. Her grandfather hadn't taken care of all her insecurities, and in that moment Jack knew he'd gladly take on the job of finishing where the old man had left off.

"Honestly?" His slightly teasing grin earned him a tiny quirk of her lips. "Honey, if you walk into my arms, I'm going to do my damnedest to make sure I earn that same dreamy look from you every time I walk into a room."

"Cocky son of a bitch," she responded on a choked sob, then launched herself across the room and into his arms.

Jack caught her high on his chest, her mouth on his, her feet inches off the floor. He took from her as long as he felt he could, then began giving back, pouring into his deep kisses all of the pent-up emotions her admission had stirred in him. Abruptly, he knew it wouldn't be enough.

"Coffee table or bed?"

It took April a few moments to understand the cryptic question. Her skin flushed deeply, but in desire, not embarrassment. "Bed."

She looked up as she said it, in time to see Jack's light eyes become swallowed in black, his pupils expanding as rapidly as his desire.

He swung her legs up onto one arm, keeping her chest crushed to his with the other, and strode to the doors leading to the bedroom. Once inside, he carried her to the foot of the queen-sized bed, then let her slid from his grip.

"Do you know how hard it was for me to leave you at your door last night?"

For the first time in what seemed like hours, April smiled. She felt wonderful, free. "Probably half as hard as it was for me to let you."

"I don't think we'll have to face that decision again."

Jack's lazy grin made her knees tremble, and all thoughts of her revelation and everything she had yet to deal with fled her mind.

It wasn't that she didn't appreciate his concerned words or perceptive insights, but right now all she wanted was to fall back onto the soft bed and pull his big, hard body down on top of hers. She wanted his lazy smiles, she wanted his wicked lips, she wanted his creative hands, and she wanted it all to herself, for as long as he'd let her have them.

At that moment she felt truly blessed, because if she wasn't mistaken, she was about to get just that.

"Why, Ms. Morgan, I do believe that was an invitation to be naughty." He crowded against her, backing her calves against the low bed frame as his hips pushed against her stomach. "I think this is a good time for a little show-and-tell."

Warming to his teasing mood, so different from their first urgent coupling, she looked up at him through her slightly lowered lashes. "Exactly how does that work, Mr. Tango?"

He raised his fingers to the neckline of her white blouse. Running just the tip of his finger inside the edge of the scoop neckline, he kept his eyes focused on hers. "I show you what I want, and you tell me how much you like it."

His voice was dark, almost hoarse, and she could have sworn his finger trembled slightly against her skin. But he just continued his lazy assault, moving on to the tender skin under her jawline, as if he had all the time in the world to wait for her answer. A shiver raced lightly down her spine as she realized that, while it wasn't forever, they did have all night.

"I . . . I think—" She sucked in her breath as his fingertip made a slow ascent along her jaw to the shell of her ear. She watched, mesmerized by his eyes, as he leaned closer, until his lips—which were hot, like his fingertips—grazed the barest part of her earlobe.

"Don't think, *mi tesoro*. Feel. Just feel." His whispered words blew intimately against her.

"I already am." She had barely gotten the words out when he gently bit her earlobe. A moan escaped her lips. He pulled the soft pad of skin into his mouth and the muscles between her legs clenched. Closer. She needed him closer. Thinking only to assuage the almost painful tightness his successive nips had created, she lifted her knee and wrapped her leg around his upper thigh.

"Sweet heaven, *corazón*," he whispered against her throat. He stilled for a moment, then yanked her other leg up around his hip and held her there. "You learn quick."

"Some things are instinctive. Show me some more, Jack." She instantly realized her request was like waving a red flag in front of a charged-up bull. The analogy pleased her and she smiled up at him. His responding grin was several degrees past wicked and she shuddered, unconsciously tightening her thighs around him.

A growling sound came from the back of his throat as he peeled her legs from his hips and let her drop to the bed. She fell softly to her back and he stood between her legs at the edge of the bed. "Show-and-tell is going to be over real quick if you aren't careful."

She said nothing, too caught up in watching his face as he looked down at her, his powers of perception peeling her outer layers away in a manner that left her far more naked than if he'd undressed her. She felt a frisson of something like fear race over her skin. What had happened between them last night had been hot and wild, but this time there would be no surrendering to the moment. She knew he meant to test her trust in him, knew he'd push her to the edge to do so.

He began to undress. It wasn't done slowly or in any sort of provocative manner. Nonetheless, she had to grip the bedcover in her fists to keep from reaching out for him. His gaze still on her, she knew he expected her to lay still.

He tossed his shirt to the floor, then unceremoniously let his shorts drop to his ankles. April couldn't have contained her gasp if her life had depended on it.

"I'm showing you how much I want you," he said, his voice rough. "Tell me how you feel."

"Very powerful." And it was the truth. Last night had been so dark, she had only felt him, big and strong inside of her. But now. Her position on the bed should have made her feel incredibly vulnerable to him, his dominance visually undeniable. Yet there was no egotism, no threat, implied or otherwise, in his stance. Instead he'd simply bared his need for her in the most honest and direct way he could, knowing how important it was to her to reestablish her trust in her own sexuality after what had happened so long ago.

Jack kneeled on the bed between her legs, no longer trusting his legs to hold him upright. Her answer was more than he'd hoped for, proving she was a lot closer to being whole than he'd credited her with. "Show me how much you need me."

He watched her slowly release the blanket wadded in her fists. Her fingers trembled, but he refrained from helping her as she fumbled with her shirt, finally yanking it free of her waistband and pulling it over her head.

Now it was his turn to gasp. Instead of a bra, she had on a filmy white camisole, her need made obvious by the way her nipples pushed at the lace that trimmed the front. She reached for the thin straps.

"Leave it on. I can see." Without asking, he reached down and pulled at the cuffs of her pants. She quickly undid the snap and zipper and lifted her hips. His heart pounded at the invitation her hips extended and he struggled to hold on to his control. He dropped her pants on the floor and looked back at her. Her gaze was riveted between his legs, and he knew she had not failed to notice his response.

Her bikinis were white and dipped down below her navel in front. He knew what she looked like, had felt her entire body inside and out the night before. Yet he didn't know her at all. Otherwise the sight of that navel wouldn't have caused him to swallow convulsively with the need to taste it. He lifted her ankle to his shoulder, determined to take the slow route, but vowing to slake that need.

April grabbed fistfuls of blanket, pulling at them in order to remain on her back. Her hips didn't want to obey, however, and when Jack lifted her other ankle to his shoulder, she shook with the effort it took to keep from bucking up.

"Reach up."

She immediately lifted her arms to him. He shook his head, his hands still gently holding her ankles.

"Reach back behind you and grab the bedposts."

Her eyes widened, but she did what he asked.

"Pull yourself back till your head hits the pillows."

She wasn't sure if what she felt was relief or disappointment. Too wired at this point to care, she pulled. He knee-walked up the bed with her, coming even farther up between her legs than before. But when she let go, he shook his head again.

"Hold on."

He'd given her the gift of the power of her own sexuality, yet she paused, trying to force her brain to make sense of the wild sensations his command sent shivering through her. The instant his teeth came into contact with the arch of her foot, she gripped the wooden posts so tightly her knuckles turned white.

Jack slowly worked his way around her ankle, dropping tiny kisses along the sensitive center line of her shin, nipping the soft flesh of her inner calf. By the time he'd reached her knee her leg was shaking so hard he made himself abandon it for the other one. When both of her legs were draped over his shoulders, twitching, he allowed himself the luxury of discovering the rest of her.

As soon as he tasted her, he felt her hands clutch the back of his head. His felt his eyes burn as he took the gift she'd given him, opening herself to him in this most vulnerable way. Smiling against her inner thigh, he pushed her bikinis aside and proceeded to make damn sure he returned the gift.

He didn't stop until her entire body bucked against him in release. Tracing small kisses up to her navel, he smiled to himself as he realized he couldn't have picked a more wonderful route to the very spot that had tempted him moments ago. He gently let her legs slide down his arms and moved up over her.

He'd wanted her eyes dreamy. They were that and more as she gazed up at him. Wonder, satisfaction, and something deeper . . . "Tell me."

She lifted her hands to his face, traced her fingers over his eyebrows, cheekbones, and lips.

"I want you, Jack Tango. Let *me* show *you*." She reached up and kissed the center of his chest, rubbing her cheek against the darker blond hair that bisected his stomach. She wriggled her hips and he quickly helped her shimmy out of her panties. Wrapping her legs around his hips, she pulled his head to hers. "Tell me what it feels like to be inside of me," she whispered in his ear.

Whatever control he had, over himself or over her, vanished. Leaning his weight on his forearms, he pushed up against her, knowing intimately just how ready she was for him, desperately seeking the words that could describe the feeling he had as he pushed into her. "Lift your legs higher; hold on to me."

She did. "Tell me, Jack."

A long groan left him as he sheathed himself inside of her. "Hot. Sweet. Tight." Each word punctuated a thrust. "Like paradise. And mine. All mine. Sweet God, April, *make me yours*." And then there were no more words.

He gave, she took. She gave, he took.

When he climaxed, he pulled her over the edge with him.

April knew she was alone even before she opened her eyes the next morning. Logically, she knew it was because Jack had told her he had lined up some shots that had to be taken at sunrise. Emotionally she knew she'd sensed his departure even in her sleep. That was why she had his pillow clutched against her chest and belly. It was a lousy substitute.

She rolled onto her back and pulled the pillow up over her eyes to shade the sun that poured in through the window behind her head. She'd wanted to go with him, to watch him work. But he'd said he'd be back before she woke up and then he'd started kissing her again and by the time they were done she had a sneaking suspicion he could come back at noon and she'd still be dozing. Where did he get the strength?

For all of two seconds she was tempted to roll back over and doze off, with scenes of last night to keep her in warm company. But the meeting was in less than three hours, according to the travel clock by the bed, so on a huge groan she forced herself to sit up. Call room service, take a hot shower, drown herself in hot tea, then work on her speech, she decided, years of scheduling her days making the thought process automatic.

Titillating visions of working in some time with Jack died when she stood and the muscles in her inner thighs protested loudly at being asked to support her weight. Glad Jack wasn't there to watch her very untitillating waddle, she gingerly made her way to the bathroom, her scheduled priorities shifting order.

Fifteen minutes later, her hair wrapped in a white hotel towel, she pulled on one of Jack's T-shirts and dialed down for some tea. If she was lucky, it would get here before they checked out tomorrow. Thankfully, she recalled Jack saying he'd bring back breakfast, so she didn't bother pushing her luck by asking for something as complex as food.

She wandered out to the small living room and settled on the couch, her muscles not protesting quite as loudly after her wonderfully steamy shower. She emptied her head of all that had transpired the night before and tried to work on her speech. Only fifteen minutes had passed before she allowed herself to admit that the stupid grin on her face had nothing to do with the plight of the local Indians, and she dropped the legal pad back on the coffee table.

She thought about getting dressed, but even with air-conditioning the room was humid and she decided it would be best to wait until it was closer to the meeting. Her gaze strayed back to the bedroom and she acknowledged with a wry grin that it would also be easier to make love with Jack if he returned in time.

The grin broadened to a smile and she pulled a throw pillow from the couch and hugged it to her body. She didn't feel awkward in the least this morning, and she knew it was because Jack had removed any and all doubts very thoroughly last night. She had no idea what lay in store for them, but for the first time in ten years she felt as if she could handle whatever life threw at her.

Wandering into the bedroom, she noticed one of Jack's nylon gear bags lying open on top of the desk. Without conscious thought, only the need to know more about what made him tick, she walked over to it. There were pictures wedged in the inside pocket, the corners poking up at odd angles, as if he'd stuffed them in there only recently. Her curiosity more than piqued, her need to look at them struggled against the knowledge of what had happened last time she'd given in to the temptation to look at his work.

Surely after what they'd shared, he wouldn't mind. Even if they were of her, she wouldn't care. Not anymore. Jack had been incredibly supportive and understanding the night before when she'd bared her ugly past. Nothing could change that, or her conviction that he was being honest with her about his reasons for being at the Cove. Besides which, she argued with herself, Jack may have done everything in his power to help her heal last night, but he kept his own problems to himself. Maybe seeing his work would help her to understand, to know what questions to ask. More than anything, she wanted to be there for him, the way he'd been there for her.

Wiping her suddenly sweaty palms against his yellow T-shirt, she gingerly slid the photos out of the pocket.

NINE

Jack balanced the paper bag and his camera gear on his left arm and opened the door to their room. "Sorry it took me so long to get back, I got caught up shooting some of the local kids playing. I hope you like fresh fruit, it's all I could—" Jack stopped dead in his tracks, clutching the brown bag tightly against his ribs, not caring if he smashed the tender fruit inside. "What are you doing?" He didn't bother to disguise his sudden unease; it was plainly obvious in his flat voice.

He was prepared for a sudden look of guilt and a hurried explanation, so the slow shifting of her attention away from the photographs she held in her hand to his face sent him reeling even further off balance. Her stunned expression knocked him down completely, rendering him incapable of speech. It wasn't possible she'd guessed the importance of those photos. *Was it?*

"Jack, these are . . ." Her speech faltered and her gaze returned to the glossy prints in her hand. He watched with something that was a cross between heightened anticipation and pain as she started to go through the small stack.

He was far enough away that the pictures themselves were little more than a blur of color, but it wasn't necessary to see them. Each one was etched in his heart in painstaking detail. He found his complete attention riveted on her face, knowing by the tiniest nuance of expression which one she was looking at. A hint of a smile, with a sad light entering her soft eyes; must be the one of the child rolling a hoop with a stick while her dog chased merrily along.

While it sounded like something from a Norman Rockwell rendering, the only similarity was the spirit of the child and possibly the dog. Her dress could only kindly be called a rag, the hoop was made out of a rusted rim from a hubcap, and the bandy-legged little dog's heritage had been blurred generations ago.

April tucked that one at the back and he saw her eyes widen a tiny fraction with pleasure. To look at her, it was as if the sparkling spray of water from the waterfall had just misted her skin. She couldn't know that a mere mile away people were blowing each other up. But Jack knew.

The next shot made Jack shift uncomfortably. A rigid bolt of lightning like a jagged slash across the glossy sheet made her stiffen, as if she'd not only heard the reverberating crash of thunder that followed but understood how humbling it was to witness the amazing power of nature.

It was as if she understood exactly how he'd felt when he'd taken the picture, his need to capture that precise moment. And yet there was no way she could understand. She had never been compelled, as he had, to become completely absorbed in something that powerful, something that far beyond the control of a human being, in order to discover the possible existence of a higher order in the chaos that was a fact of life on earth.

But somehow she did. He stilled as she put that one aside, then felt his blood run hot as she absorbed the impact of the next one. The unguarded look of desire that flashed across her face involved him as completely as her previous expression had. *My God!* She did know. She understood.

"April, come here." He moved to stand next to her even as he spoke. She didn't look up, didn't give any indication she'd even heard his hoarse plea, and he fought down the urge to pull her into his arms.

He knew the photo was simply of a bird and

a flower. Most people would have appreciated the rich color of the crimson hibiscus, maybe have been amused at the rapid beating of the tiny humming-bird's wings. But that's not why he'd waited hours for that shot. And one look at her rapidly dilating pupils told him she knew why he'd chosen that instant in time to release the shutter.

He knew he saw the crystalline morning dew beaded on each soft vermilion petal. She felt the quiver of the tiny wings as intimately as if they'd brushed against her skin. She responded in an elemental way, as he had, to the long, spearlike beak, brought into sharp focus as it thrust into the center of the exotic bloom in search of life-giving nectar. Jack stared hard at her, shaken beyond action by her response to his work, his vision. He willed her to look at him, and very slowly she tilted her gaze to meet his.

Nothing he'd ever photographed in his life, or would from that point on, would ever match what he found in her eyes. Respect, desire, a deep yearn-ing. All those things were there. But it was the innate understanding, shining as clearly as a beacon on a storm, welcoming him inside, telling him that, yes, she'd found the other half of herself in him as well.

Raising a shaky hand to cup her chin, he dropped a heartbreakingly gentle kiss on her lips. *I love you, April Marie Morgan de la Torre.* He wanted to whisper the words out loud, but his throat had closed the second she'd looked at him.

Desire quickly eclipsed all the other emotions swirling in her eyes, except the one he had to believe was her love for him. Dropping his parcels and camera gear on the table, he pulled the now-forgotten photos from her hands and lifted her into his arms. Nuzzling her neck as he walked toward the bed, he managed to say, "How late can you be for that meeting?"

"It's not for hours," she whispered back, her hand tracing a delicate line over his face.

He sat on the edge of the bed with her in his lap, letting her continue her sensual tactile exploration of his face. It was as if she was truly seeing each feature for the first time.

He found he didn't mind, even if her inspection did make him smile a bit self-consciously. His soul had just been completely exposed to her and he realized that he should feel nervous. Maybe the fact that he wasn't proved he was truly in love with her. His trust ran so deep that just knowing his soul was in her tender care made him feel more free and relaxed than he'd been in his entire adult life.

"What exactly are you looking at?" he queried softly, grabbing her fingers and kissing their tips softly.

Her brown eyes bore into his, demanding total attention. "I think I'm looking at a man who has had to work increasingly harder at finding the beauty in a world slowly going mad. A man who has, by the nature of his work, had to bury the very sensitivity that makes him so good at his job, in order to survive without losing his own sanity."

His lips stilled on her fingers, his eyes frozen on hers. There was no pity in their warm depths, only a trace of compassion from someone who'd been forced to make her own serenity, build her own beauty, when her own world was torn apart and made too ugly to survive in.

"And you heal me," he whispered, his breath mingling with hers. "When I came down here, I wasn't sure what the problem was. Or if I even had one. But I did. And catching up on sleep and taking time out from the pressure isn't the answer. I don't know if I can go back to that kind of life, April. What I do know is that with you I feel like the search for my own peace has ended."

He pulled her arm around his neck and fell back on the bed, pulling her down on top of him. His kisses were fiercely gentle at first, but as she responded with a quiet fervor of her own he became more and more demanding, until he tore at her clothes and she at his because they couldn't be close enough.

"Love me, Jack."

"*Sí, mi tesoro, mi corazón.* Always." Jack pulled her under him and pushed into her in one fluid thrust. She bucked against him, meeting him thrust for thrust, gasping his name over and over until they both rode right over the edge.

April held on to the loose door handle of the pickup truck in a vain effort to save her sore backside a few extra bruises. She glanced over at Jack, who somehow felt her gaze and shot her a quick wink before returning his attention to the rutted road that led back to the Cove. A small smile crossed her face as she realized her achy tenderness couldn't all be blamed on bad shocks.

"You look like the proverbial cat," Jack said. "Of course after that heartrending speech you gave yesterday afternoon, you deserve to."

If he hadn't specifically mentioned the time, she might have questioned which speech he was referring to: the one she made to him in their room after seeing his photos, or the one she gave to the committee later that day. Her smile broadened as she recalled the looks on the officials' faces. Prejudice against the local Zapotecs and other Indians wouldn't be overcome easily, but she felt she'd made some headway by gaining the bureaucrats' agreement to allow her to continue to hire them.

She glanced back at Jack, smiling as she recalled the way he'd hounded her with endless questions about the area, the meeting, and the plight of the local tribes. He'd seemed truly interested in her struggle to help them. "*Your* smile might be considered a bit smug as well."

"Hey, I just spent two days, almost all of it in bed—" At her raised eyebrows he laughed and added, "Well, we usually made it to the bed. And I was with the most incredible woman I've ever met. You're lucky I'm not singing."

Except for a change in gender, April had been thinking the same thing, but hearing him say it made her pulse speed up in a delicious spiral. Could she actually love this man? A man on the verge of making life-changing decisions? Decisions that could very well not include her, regardless of what he felt, or thought he felt, now? She was very much afraid the answer to all of it was a loud, resounding yes!

"Getting hot, *mi tesoro*?" he said, his smile on full-charm. "Your skin is turning the most wonderful shade of pink. Maybe we should find some shade somewhere and see if I can't cool you down."

April laughed as she looked at the dry, dusty landscape all around them. "Why do you think I went to so much expense to specially design Paradise Cove to support all that lush tropical foliage? The only shade between here and there is inside the cab of this truck."

"Might be a little cramped but—"

"Jack!" April tried for indignant but her laugh

ruined it. Besides, it would require an Oscar-winning performance to act shocked at anything he could toss at her after spending a good portion of the last two days naked in bed with the man. "I've already been away almost two days. As it is Carmen is probably frantic and I'm sure—"

"You know perfectly well you've trained your people so well that the resort could almost run itself." He looked over at her and laughed at the mock look of indignation on her face. "Hey, that was a compliment, you know. Besides, I did say 'almost,' didn't I?"

After their laughter faded, they settled into a comfortable silence for the next twenty minutes or so, and even the jolting ride couldn't prevent April from allowing her mind to drift into figuring out how they might possibly make their relationship work. What Jack said about the resort almost running itself was true to a degree. And after their talk the day she'd found his pictures, it seemed as if he was looking for a change. But even if he didn't return to the same type of journalism, it didn't mean he wasn't planning on returning to the States. After all, everything else he had was there. Friends, family, other job opportunities. Everything. Everything but her.

For the first time in years, April wondered what it would be like to go back herself. It had been such a long time, she thought, but with Jack by her side she knew she'd be strong enough to face her old ghosts. All thoughts of the upcoming presidential race and Markham's possible bid slid from her mind. The thought of his gaining any more power sickened her, but after all, she could hardly change things by coming forward with ten-year-old claims that had only managed to destroy her the first time around.

Surely she could go back to the States with Jack and maintain her anonymity, she told herself. And with his type of work, surely they could work out some arrangement to spend time in both Mexico and the States.

"Do you ever think about contacting your father?"

The question gave her a start at the same time the truck hit a bump, and her head knocked against the door frame. The pain that shot through her head effectively wiped out the shock of his unexpected question.

"Are you okay? I didn't mean to startle you. I guess I was wrapped up in my thoughts and didn't realize how that would sound."

"I'm okay," she answered, absently rubbing her scalp until the slight pain receded. "You did startle me, but I guess it's a fair question." She didn't tell him how her own thoughts had strangely paralleled his. "I didn't for a long time. But after Grandpa Morgan died, I gave it a lot of thought. Paradise

Cove was well on its way to becoming a success and I wasn't as threatened by the idea of my father's power."

"But you didn't." It wasn't phrased as a question.

"No, you're right, I didn't. But it wasn't out of fear, or even residual anger. I even understand, given his background, how he came to the conclusions he did. I just can't seem to get past the sense of betrayal." She shifted to look at Jack. "Aside from my grandfather, who was thousands of miles away, my father was all I had left, Jack, and he threw me to the wolves. I guess I can't forgive him for that."

"I can understand, *mi tesoro*. I don't see my dad or my brother much, but just knowing they are there for me is sort of grounding. A sense of home, I guess. It just seems like such a waste for both of you." She turned back to face the window. "I won't mention it again."

They rode for several more miles and April tried hard to mentally recapture the light, teasing mood that up to that point had been a part of their return trip. Her thoughts seemed doomed to stay dark, though, as she helplessly found herself counting the number of days Jack had left at the resort. All the negative questions she'd forced from her mind regarding where they would go from that point surfaced, threatening to swamp her. Did he even want her to go back with him? Would he want to try and find a way to make their relationship work?

The sudden swerving of the truck onto the side of the road jolted her out of her painful thoughts. "What are you doing? Did we blow a tire?"

"The tires are fine. And before you ask, we have plenty of gas."

"Then why did you pull over like it was some dire emergency?"

"Because it was. It is."

His oblique answers did nothing for her sudden need to unleash her temper, but he spoke before she could explode.

"Is Carmen expecting us back at a real specific time?"

"No. She and I both know better than to try to stay to any kind of exact schedule regarding travel in Mexico. Why?"

"Because," he said softly as he grabbed her hand. He opened his door and pulled her across to the edge of the seat.

"Okay, I give. Because why?"

"Look." He turned and pointed to an outcropping of rock that thrust over a slight decline pointing toward the ocean. "I found us some shade. Rest-stop time."

Turning back, he stared at her, smiling and shielding his eyes from the bright midday sun with his hand. After a long moment she answered him with a slow smile of her own. She put her hands on his shoulders, intent on hopping down, but he put his hands on hers, stopping her.

"The ground has too many loose rocks. Here." He turned and presented his back to her.

"Here, what?"

"Are we going to stand around doing bad Laurel and Hardy impressions all day or do you want a piggyback ride?"

"Well, why didn't you just say so?"

He chuckled and reached back, but she didn't hop right on. "Now what?" he asked over his shoulder.

"Well, my shoes might not be made for rock climbing, but this skirt is definitely not made for piggyback rides."

He turned and April knew she should've jumped down at the first sight of the wicked grin on his face, but his big hands clamped down on her thighs, blocking her escape. Jack made a quick survey of the road, knowing full well there probably wouldn't be another car for an hour, then slid his hands, and her skirt, up to her hips. Pretending not to hear her sudden gasp, he turned and backed up until his jean-clad rear end was pushed up against her silk bikini underwear. He reached back and pulled her legs around his hips. "Hold on."

She did. And when he issued that same command some minutes later in the protective shadow of the large boulders, she didn't have to be told twice.

As she turned onto the pathway to Jack's bungalow, April reached up and pulled the ebony stick from her hair, then quickly finger-raked the tangles loose. Smiling like an idiot and not caring who noticed, she hopped up the steps onto the porch.

They'd been back for five days. And five glorious nights. Jack had insisted on keeping his bungalow, which had initially made her wonder if he'd wanted to distance himself from her now that they were back. He hadn't let her wonder for long. And now she had to admit she kind of liked the challenge of reworking her schedule to fit in surprise visits to the intimate hut.

She'd looked around the grounds, but hadn't spied Jack anywhere. "He just has to be here," she whispered fervently. She had finagled an entire hour off and she refused to spend it alone. She forcibly pushed away the thought that Jack's vacation time was nearing an end. Just because he hadn't actually said he was staying didn't mean anything. Neither had he said he was leaving, she firmly reminded herself as she pushed the screen door open.

"Jack?" Her call met with silence, but her grin

broadened as she heard the unmistakable sounds of the shower. She recalled the day, which now seemed light-years ago, that she had faced down a dripping wet, barely clad Jack over the photos he'd taken of her at the wedding. It all seemed so ridiculous now. Now she knew he'd never hurt her.

Deciding that she could use a quick shower herself, she stepped toward the bathroom door, only to stop short at a sudden rapping on the door behind her. She whirled around and found Dom smiling at her.

While she hadn't made any secret of her relationship with Jack, she had really thought she'd managed to sneak away unnoticed. But she knew Dom would handle himself professionally, so she did as well. Smiling brightly, as if she were in the middle of her office instead of a guest's private bungalow, she said, "Hi, Dom. What's up?"

"*Hola, Señorita* April. There is no problem. I have mail for Jack. He asked for me to bring it right away."

"Thank you. I'll make sure he gets it right away." A trace of uneasiness crept into the older man's expression, surprising April. Assuming he was merely taking his responsibility seriously, she hastened to assure him, "I'll tell him you delivered it yourself. Thank you, Dom." Her words hadn't relieved the man, but her tone, though kind, made it clear that his responsibility was done. She took the flat brown folder from his hands, careful not to dislodge the yellow note tucked into the band that secured it shut.

"*Gracias, señorita.* Please tell *Señor* Jack that the envelope was badly torn when it arrived and Eva tossed it out. I am so sorry."

Aha, so that was the problem. "Don't worry about it, Dom. I can't see how that will hurt."

Dom nodded and April watched him turn and move down the path in what was almost a trot. Her smile faded as quickly as her curiosity over her concierge's odd behavior, her attention immediately drawn back to the banded folder.

What in the world had Jack been expecting? She stiffened suddenly. Was this from Franklin? It might even be his next assignment. Feeling her knees begin to wobble at the unwanted intrusion of Jack's other life, she made her way to the small couch and plopped down, resting the folder on her knees.

The urge to look inside ate at her. Surely Jack would tell her what was inside when he looked at it. There was no need for her to look. April's curiosity waged an intense war with her trust in Jack until she realized she'd worried the yellow note that had been tucked under the band into a wadded ball in her fist.

"Oops." She hurriedly began smoothing it out against the flat surface of the folder, but stilled as she saw her name scrawled across one line in unfamiliar handwriting.

Any doubts as to her right to read the note disappeared. If it was about her, she had every right to read it. Smoothing the rest of the wrinkles as best she could, she began reading:

Jack,

Leave it to you to find the story of the century in the middle of nowhere! I should have known better than to think you've actually been resting down there. How on earth did you manage to locate April de la Torre, for God's sake? At first I thought you had gone off the deep end when you had me check out that old Texan, Smithson. You could have provided me with a few more details, but I'm sure you had your reasons. After all, I guess it isn't easy to hide an investigation from the CEO of the resort.

No, she thought wildly, resisting the urge to tear the damning note to shreds. Jack wouldn't do this to me. There must be an explanation. Forcing the bile back down her throat, she made herself finish the letter, praying that she'd understand by the time she got to the end.

I'm honored that you thought enough of my investigative skills to put two and two together. The word is that Markham is very close to announcing his bid—I hope the postal service gets this to you in time. You scoop him early on in the race and you're looking at another Pulitzer, my friend. Vaya con Dios, buddy, Frank

April tossed the note to the floor as if it had burned her fingers. Fighting to keep calm, trying desperately to find any rational explanation, she lurched up from the couch and paced to the bedroom door, then back to the front door. The urge to run was very strong and she felt all of her old self-preservation instincts rush back to the fore.

She distantly realized that the shower was no longer running and she knew that she couldn't leave without facing Jack. Not without hearing his side of the story.

She turned away from the door and found Jack lounging in the doorway to the bedroom, the white towel draping his hips forming a strong contrast to his tanned chest.

He said nothing, but his expression made it clear he knew something was terribly wrong. Using every last scrap of control she had, she calmed her breathing and schooled her expression into one that announced it was willing to listen.

"While you were in the shower, Dom brought the mail you were expecting. He, uh . . ." She felt her eyes burn and she took a deep breath to steady her voice. "The envelope was ruined. Franklin stuck a note to you under the flap. I wouldn't have read it, but I saw my name and . . ."

Jack levered himself off the door frame and walked to the couch a few feet from where she stood. She silently handed him the folder, then crossed her arms.

"Where's the note, April?"

"On the couch." She'd expected him to grab it and read it. Instead he just put the folder on the couch on top of the crumpled note, then turned back to face her again.

"What could Franklin have said to make you this upset? The information in that folder was stuff I requested ages ago, after the wedding."

April's eyes widened in shock. It was true then? He'd been digging as far back as the wedding? Her mind ran wild. Had he somehow been responsible for her photographer leaving so he could neatly fill in?

Finally Jack snapped. He lunged for her and grabbed her arms. "What in the hell is wrong with you? I can't help you unless you tell me!"

She turned glassy eyes at him, then dropped them to his grip on her arms. "Let me go."

"So you can run? No. You tell me first what has got you so scared."

"Let me go, Jack. I'm not going anywhere until you explain why in the hell you've been having me investigated."

He dropped her arms, but didn't step away from her. She forced herself to hold his gaze, but she didn't see guilt there. If she wasn't mistaken she saw anger, with a good bit of hurt thrown in as well.

"Why would I do that? You had to know that when you told me in Oaxaca what happened, it was the first time I'd heard it. After all we've shared together, what else is there for me to dig up?"

April paled at his tautly controlled tone. "You said yourself you asked Franklin for this. Maybe you didn't think your plan to seduce the information out of me would work and this was backup. But it doesn't change the fact that you're investigating me, Jack."

"If you'd stop for two seconds you'd realize how ridiculous you sound."

April's skin zoomed from pasty white to flushed red. "Well, I'm sorry if you think keeping my private life private, after the hell you people put me through the last time, is ridiculous. I don't happen to think so." She spun around, but Jack's hand clamped down on her arm, stopping her in her tracks.

"Oh, no you don't. You said you aren't leaving until you hear the whole story, and by damn you're staying if I have to tie you to the couch."

Abruptly April relaxed, her burst of anger spending itself like a brilliant rocket on the Fourth of July. She resigned herself to listening to him, wanting only to expedite leaving this bungalow so she could go somewhere private, if there was such a place around the resort, to lick her wounds.

Feeling her resignation, Jack gentled his grip

but didn't release her completely. He knew the only way he could get through to her now was to weaken the defenses she was rapidly piling up between them, so he used her initial lapse to tug her into his arms.

She struggled, but he shushed her, whispering quietly against her hair. She stilled, and though she didn't return his embrace, just the knowledge that she'd still allow him to touch her, to be this close to her, gave him the strength he needed to try and sort this mess out.

"My reasons for asking Franklin for the information were personal, not business. But, honey, I've heard the story already from your own lips, and while I may be sick over what Markham and your father did to you . . . Actually, if I saw either one right now I'd gladly wring their necks. But the fact is that it was ten years ago. What could I possibly gain from writing about it now? Other than a where-is-she-now story—and I'd like to think you know me well enough to realize I don't do that kind of thing—you really aren't newsworthy."

Instead of the relief he'd expected to feel under the fingers he was trailing up and down her spine, he felt her stiffen further, a feat he hadn't thought possible.

She lifted her head from his chest and looked him straight in the eyes, her expression nothing less than challenging.

"Are you telling me that you didn't ask Franklin to find the connection between Smithson and Markham?"

Jack's confused reaction lasted approximately two seconds. He'd missed something terribly important here. He should have known she wouldn't lose it like this without strong provocation. "I saw you and Smithson talking at the reception. Something he said spooked you. At the time I was merely curious and wondered if he was the reason you were so skittish around me."

She tried to pull from his arms but his arms tightened around her. She burrowed against his chest, but he butted his forehead gently against hers until she looked up at him. Then he said, "What did Franklin find out? What didn't you tell me, April?"

"Markham is about to announce his candidacy for president. Apparently he's a heavy favorite. With all the hoopla over morality and family values lately, Franklin thinks you're on to something. Apparently he thinks that if I come out of seclusion and go public with the charges again, it will knock him out of the race. And, it goes without saying, the journalist with the scoop wins the prize."

"Holy hell." He pulled her against his chest again, trying to block out the doubt in her eyes while he quickly tried to figure out what to do.

Because his emotions were irrevocably entwined with her, he had to work hard to think rationally, to sort out what should be done.

Taking a steadying breath, he looked back down at her. "You do know that I had no idea." After a long pause during which he was certain he would die for lack of oxygen, she answered him.

"I want to believe that more than I've ever wanted to believe anything in my whole life."

"Well, you can believe it, dammit! Because it's the truth. Are you ready for another truth?" He didn't wait for an answer; it was now or never. "I love you, April. Do you hear me? I love you, dammit!"

Shocked at the burning sensation behind his eyes, he lowered his head the rest of the way and kissed her long and hard until they were both wavering on their feet. Sucking in a lungful of air, he broke away a mere fraction of an inch and whispered raggedly against her lips, "I'd sooner die than hurt you. Don't you know I'll do everything I can to make sure the slime pays this time?"

It took a few moments for his words to register; his declaration, combined with the kiss, had effectively muddled her brain. It must have, because he couldn't have just said what she thought he had. She ripped herself from his arms, backing quickly away from him, her arms outstretched in front of her, palms up. "You think I'm going to come forward again?" she all but shrieked. "Why, Jack? You said yourself it was old news."

"He's running for the goddamn presidency, April! Can you tell me you're just going to sit down here in your safe little haven and let a rapist take over the White House?"

"And what am I supposed to do?" She wrapped her arms around her waist as the anguish over her impotence to change the situation washed over her again. "He'll just crush me again. The evidence hasn't changed."

"Then I'll find more. April, I'm damn good at what I do. I'll find Frannie. Together maybe we can get her to confess. It's too late to press charges, but at the least we'll stop his campaign. Let me talk to your father. Maybe he's had a change of heart."

April felt chilled to the bone as she watched Jack transform magically before her eyes into the prize-winning photojournalist that he truly was. He was wrong, though; her father would never change. And finding Frannie after all this time was statistically more difficult than finding the proverbial needle.

It wasn't her inability to nail Markham that deadened her, however. It was realizing beyond a shadow of a doubt that Jack Tango wasn't ready to make the change to a quieter, less stress-filled life. The man standing before her, even wrapped in nothing more than a damp bath towel, fairly radiated excitement. The challenge of getting the story burned so strongly in his eyes they almost sparked.

She forced herself to stand there for a moment and absorb the impact of him, the power that emanated from him, the sensuality that even now, with her dreams nothing more than smashed fragments scattered at her feet, made her body respond to him.

"April?" Her name on his lips was both a question and a plea. She should have known he'd see her decision in her eyes.

"No, Jack. If you really knew me, you'd never ask me to help. I would have gladly gone back with you, but not for a story. Not for that story. Do what you have to, but you'll have to do it without me."

"To hell with the damn story!" Jack yelled, his temper frayed to the snapping point. "But it is precisely because I do know you that I didn't think I *had* to ask. I actually thought you'd *want* to go back. The April Morgan I know has worked damn hard to become a strong, independent woman. Strong enough to do whatever she has to to put her past behind her, once and for all. If you're going to waste this opportunity, then maybe you're right. Maybe I don't know you at all." Jack's expression was closed, his tone more cold than accusing.

April absorbed his stinging rejection without flinching, all the while praying her control would see her past the door. "I *have* put it all behind me," she said, her voice barely louder than a whisper. "But if going back to the States to dig up useless pain and relive hellish memories best left forgotten is the price tag for being with you, I simply can't afford it. Good-bye, Jack," she said quietly, then turned and left.

Two painfully long and silent days later, he was gone.

TEN

April turned up the familiar path to Jack's old bungalow, determined to go in this time and not stop on the front porch. He'd been gone for over a week and she still hadn't let the cleaning crew touch the private hut. She had no delusions that he was coming back, and she knew it wasn't healthy, and it was certainly a poor decision from a business standpoint, but she had kept the bungalow empty since he'd left.

Which was why she was here, she told herself. To, once and for all, rid herself of the ghost of Jack Tango and get on with her life. Such as it was.

Rearranging her office and swapping desks with Carmen had taken care of one ghost. Now she would put this one to rest, too. Dry-eyed, she slipped her master keycard into the slot and let herself into the bungalow.

At first glance it looked like all the other bungalows. Her laugh was humorless. "What were you expecting? A note?" she asked the stale air. As if in answer, her gaze fell on the couch and she felt her breath leave her body in a whoosh.

On the couch, exactly where he'd laid it one week earlier, was the brown folder. She quickly checked the rest of the place, but it was empty of all of Jack's belongings. Unsure of the symbolism of his leaving the folder behind, but certain it had been intentional, she picked it up. Under it was the crumpled letter from Franklin. She stared at it for a full minute. Then she sat down on the small couch, opened the folder, and began to read.

A full hour later, April put the folder aside and stood. Arching her back to work out the kinks, she stretched, then simply stood there, her mind a whirlwind that couldn't settle on a single train of thought.

Franklin had been very thorough; she could see why Jack respected the man. Not only had he made the connection between Smithson, Markham, and herself, but he'd even included some recent information regarding her father. It was that information that had sent her mind into a tailspin.

The information was dry, mainly details of his recent business dealings and whom he'd aligned himself with politically. But it was the first time she'd read anything about him in ten years, the first time he'd reached out in any way and touched her, even if it was through a third party. She smiled sadly as she wondered if he'd aged gracefully, then laughed at her imaginings. Of course he had. Her father had been the typical Latino male, full of charm, sure of himself, and always in control. He wouldn't dare let the vagaries of time affect him adversely.

Feeling strangely melancholy, April perched again on the couch, seemingly unable, once the floodgates had opened, to stop thinking about him. For years she had felt as if she had no family, and not without cause. But her abrupt departure had left him all alone too. She groaned. "Next thing I know I'll actually feel sorry for the old man." And in that split second her anger left her, and tears she hadn't been aware of holding back slid down her cheeks. The tears turned to sobs and April simply wrapped her arms around her waist and let them flow unchecked.

When she couldn't cry over the past any longer, she stood and left the bungalow. Minutes later she entered her office and instructed a very stunned Carmen to place a call to her father in the States and, if she couldn't get through, to keep trying until she did. Then she went into her office and began methodically organizing the matters on her desk, quickly deciding who would be best to handle each problem until she returned. She was going home.

Jack very gently placed the receiver back on the base, then stared across his paper-strewn desk at a clearly excited Franklin.

"So? Don't drag this out. Was it the right Frannie this time?"

Jack raked his fingers through his already rumpled hair and took another sip of lukewarm coffee. He needed a shower, sleep, and a cold beer—preferably in that order. But that would have to wait. "Yes, it was."

"Bingo! I knew you could do it!" Franklin spun around in his chair and let out a wild whoop. He stopped abruptly and braced his hands on the desk. "Will she talk?"

"Probably." Jack looked away from the glazed excitement in his friend's eyes. At the moment he couldn't imagine ever having that much enthusiasm for anything ever again. Unless, of course, it was three days of uninterrupted sleep. Sleep. Even the scant hours he'd managed to see a bed since his return to L.A. two weeks ago had been a joke. Hard as he tried, he couldn't shake the idea that he shouldn't be alone in bed anymore. He missed April.

The haunted, hunted look that had entered her eyes when he'd blindly assumed she would step forward was the only thing preventing him from just getting up and walking out. Out for good. Out somewhere, anywhere. Anywhere where he didn't hear April's voice, smell her perfume, look up when someone with dark curly hair passed him on the street, even though he knew each and every time it wouldn't be her. It would never be her. "Dammit!"

Franklin started at his outburst. "What, what?" After a moment of silence a knowing look came into Franklin's eyes. For all his enthusiasm over bringing new light to the old charges against Markham, Franklin hadn't been blind to Jack's obvious reluctance to do the story. "You want me to talk to her?"

Jack thought for a minute, sorely tempted to just turn the whole thing over to Franklin. But he knew he wouldn't. Not because he didn't trust him to do the job, but because he had to trust himself enough to see this through. If Frannie would come forward, they could take care of Markham's bid without having to do more than mention April's initial role, and then it would be as heroine, not villain. And Jack was firmly convinced he was the only man for that job.

"No. I'll do it since I made the contact." He paused again, then said, "But I do want you to do one thing for me."

"Name it."

"When the story comes out, I want it under your byline." Jack went on over Franklin's very vocal objections. "Just trust me that it's better this way. Okay?"

"Against my better judgment, okay. But I reserve the right to try and change your mind. Deal?"

A weary smile creased Jack's face. "Deal." Before they could begin to map out a strategy, the phone on Jack's desk jangled. He scooped it up and leaned his forehead on his other fist. "Tango."

When the other caller identified himself, Jack slowly lifted his head, his expression a mixture of wariness and restrained hope. He listened, answering yes and no when necessary, then hung up. Very slowly he allowed an honest smile to curve his lips.

"Who in the hell put that look on your face? If I didn't know better I'd guess Ed McMahon."

"Even better." He spun his chair around and looked out of his office window at the barely visible noonday L.A. skyline. "That was April's father. She's going to be interviewed on television tomorrow morning, live."

"Well, I'll be damned. Hoisted by our own petard." Franklin fell silent for a moment, then asked, "You don't seem to be too bothered over being scooped out of the story of the year, or at least of the election—and by a former lover at that. You must be slipping, *mi amigo*."

Jack spun around so quickly he had to grab the edge of his desk. His eyes had narrowed; his voice was hard and flat. "Franklin, we've been colleagues for eleven years and friends for over ten. But I won't be held responsible for what happens if you ever speak of her with anything less than respect."

Instead of being cowed by Jack's threat, Franklin grinned and slapped his hand against his thigh. "So that's the way the wind blows. I knew there was more to your surly moods and general grumpiness than too much work and lack of sleep. Those are the staples of life for you anyway. So, are you going to be there?"

"I'm in L.A. and the interview is in New York. I still can't believe she contacted her father, much less left Mexico," he added, more to himself than his friend.

"She and her old man made amends?"

"I don't think I'd go that far. But from what Mr. de la Torre said, at least they're talking again." Jack stood and walked over to the small corner table to refresh his coffee. He took one sip, spit it back in the cup, tossed it in the trash, then turned back to his desk, swearing under his breath.

"Go to her."

"I don't know," Jack answered shortly, irritated with the uncustomary indecision that plagued him whenever the decision at hand had to do with April. "I know what this is costing her, and I'm afraid my presence there is the last thing she needs right now."

"She doesn't have to know. You'll know. That's what counts." Franklin stood and leaned over the desk to lay a hand on Jack's shoulder. "And don't give me any crap about the time zones. That's why they call them 'red-eye' flights." He chuckled at the rueful look Jack shot him and added, "And I bet if you flash your red beauties at the ticket counter, the agent will let you on for half price. At least you can get some sleep on the plane."

And just like that Jack knew he was going. Franklin was right, April didn't have to know he was there. But in case she needed him—for what he didn't know—he had to be there.

But first he had to make a few phone calls, call in a few favors, then pay a visit to a certain Frannie Stine-White.

April nervously adjusted the mike attached to her collar. She shivered despite the bright lights aimed at her, forcing her mind to review what she wanted to say.

As part of the agreement for the interview, she'd set some strict guidelines as to the content of the questions. The interviewer was well aware that if she tried to direct the conversation into areas April had expressly stated she wouldn't discuss, she'd simply stand up and leave. And she knew there was nothing an interviewer feared more than dead airtime.

She glanced across the small soundstage at her father, still unable to believe he was here. As she'd expected, his Latin heritage had held him in good stead. But upon closer inspection, April had seen the lines around his eyes, the sadness in the tight corners of his mouth. She was still a long way from coming to terms with what he had done to her, but loneliness had apparently been a two-way street, and time had been a teacher to him as well as her. She had hope, and for now, that was enough.

The interviewer, a perky blonde who had all of America extolling her many virtues, took the seat next to April's and adjusted her own mike. "Don't be nervous," she said, adding a wry smile. "I know, easier said and all that, but I've done this many times. I promise I'll make it as easy on you as I can." She turned for a last minute touch-up from the makeup woman.

April used the moment to flash a quick smile at her father and then schooled her features into what she hoped was a polished smile befitting the CEO of a successful resort. She quashed the untimely surge of need for a specific light-eyed smile. You don't need Jack to hold your hand, she lectured herself as she allowed one of the crew to adjust her chair slightly. This is your decision and yours alone, and it's the right one. *And he'd known it all along*.

"All set?"

April tucked her sudden need for Jack into the back of her mind—admitting it would never fade completely—and faced the camera. "Ready as I'll ever be."

Jack kept to the far reaches of the brightly lit studio, hoping the lights would go down soon. He forced his gaze away from April and turned to the woman standing beside him.

Small-statured with light brown hair and a ready smile, Frannie Stine-White had been a pleasant surprise. The intervening years had been more than good to her. Her job as a lobbyist on Capitol Hill for a labor organization had given her immeasurable self-confidence. Jack couldn't have picked a better witness if he'd trained one himself.

When he'd approached her about coming forward, she had seemed almost relieved to talk to him. Appearing on national television had been another matter entirely, though. As weary as he'd been, it had taken all of Jack's considerable charm to persuade her to come to New York. He'd had to promise her anonymity if she agreed to be interviewed. The network had been more than eager to grant that request and any other.

She'd refused payment of any kind, simply wanting her story to be told. No charges were going to be pressed. Her goal was the same as April's—to keep Markham out of the White House.

The network had tried to get Jack to talk, but he had given them a very firm no and they'd been wise enough not to push.

"Are you okay?" he asked her in hushed tones.

"I guess. Do you think I'll have a chance to speak with April when this is done? I'd really like to tell her how much I appreciate being given the chance to tell my story, and to apologize for not being able to before."

Jack understood Frannie's need to see April, but he couldn't guarantee anything. He told her as much, then escorted her to the private room the network had set up for her portion of the interview.

After she'd gone, and after receiving whispered assurances from her that she would be fine, Jack finally allowed himself to look at April again. The effect she had on him hadn't lessened over time. In fact, if the heat that now rocked his body was any indication, it had actually increased.

It took considerable restraint to stay put and not go to her. He knew she'd been told about Frannie. He could only hope his orders had been followed and that his name had been kept out of it. He'd asked that she be told Frannie had come forward on her own. He wasn't taking any chances that she'd misconstrue his actions in some way and cancel the interview.

The lights dimmed and the interviewer introduced her special guest. The next fifteen minutes were the longest ones of Jack's life. When the lights came back up, the crew applauded April, and he even noticed a few people making suspicious swipes at their eyes. He wasn't surprised; his own felt a bit gritty.

Suddenly, as if she'd sensed his presence, she looked directly at him, or at least in his direction. Jack's gut twisted with mixed feelings. Part of him wanted to storm over to her, pull her into his arms, and kiss her until she agreed that they belonged together no matter what. But the part of him which understood that her rejection of him in the bungalow that day went further than just her refusal to risk pride by coming forward, made him step farther back into the shadows.

He watched intently as she scanned the area, then let out a sigh of relief when she was finally distracted by another crew member. Jack pictured for the thousandth time the sudden perception that had crept onto her face just before she'd said good-bye. She'd known then that he hadn't resolved the questions still plaguing him regarding his own future. And because he had no right to force her to make a decision until he'd made a few of his own, he'd let her go.

But seeing her again without talking to her, without touching her, had taken a far bigger toll on him than he'd expected. She laughed in response to something one of the crew said and Jack felt his control slip past the point of danger. He knew then, without a shred of doubt, that his decision had been made. Quietly slipping out the side door, he hailed a cab to take him to the airport.

April turned the corner past the covered parking lot and headed toward the main gate about a quarter mile down the paved road. The newspapers her father had promised to send detailing the demise of Markham's career should be arriving today and she didn't want to wait in her office for them to be delivered. At least she told herself that was the cause of her restlessness. "I'm not going to think about him today," she muttered, then smiled ruefully. She'd made herself that promise every morning for the past two weeks, and she hadn't succeeded yet.

Forcing her thoughts back to the papers she was expecting, she permitted a small smile to cross her face as she anticipated reading about the very public scrutiny Markham's private life was under right now. Doing the right thing, rather than revenge, had been her motive in speaking out, but she knew she'd be less than human if she didn't admit that a small part of her relished his downfall, at least for one afternoon's worth of reading.

Her smile faded a bit, becoming more tentative as her thoughts turned to her father's impending visit. She wanted him to see what she'd done with his late father-in-law's once-fledgling business, though she suspected now that he'd kept track of her all along. Their reconciliation had a long way to go, but his solid support during her brief visit to the States had provided a strong base on which to build.

Unavoidably, her memory of her trip to New York made her think of Jack.

She couldn't help but wonder what he thought of her coming back to do the interview. She realized now how strongly she'd hoped he'd contact her, or somehow let her know he'd seen her and approved of what she'd done. She'd been tempted to try and at least track down Franklin to see if he knew where Jack had been assigned, but in the end she had spent a week with her father, then flown back to Mexico.

Even in that short time away, she'd realized that Paradise Cove had truly become home to her, not just a safe haven. And as long as Jack was trotting the globe, trailing after another story, and her life was in Mexico, running the resort, she had no right to try and involve herself in his life again.

Head down, her mind wandered helplessly back over the weeks they'd spent together. Her gaze was focused loosely on the ground in front of her feet, so she heard him before she saw him. A harsh grunt reached her ears, but it didn't register that someone was coming toward her on the road until she heard the string of expletives that followed. She looked up, and the sight that greeted her eyes stopped her dead in her tracks, made her afraid to even breathe for fear that she'd break the spell she must surely be under.

Her first impulse was to rub her eyes, certain the heat and her constant thoughts of him had conjured up a mirage that just looked like Jack. But in a split second his crystalline-green eyes were locked on hers and she knew he was really there. So close it would take barely a dozen steps to reach his side, to touch him, taste him.

But she didn't do any of those things, couldn't. The visceral impact he had on her senses kept her still as a stone. He was stripped to the waist; the golden hair curling against the darkened skin of his chest did little to stop the beads of sweat which trickled over his ridged abdomen before being absorbed into the waistband of his dusty jeans. His hands were still braced on the tailgate of the truck, and she found herself intensely aware of the vein that snaked its way down his biceps.

She'd dreamed about his coming back every night for weeks; what he'd look like, what he'd say, what she would say. But now that he was here she couldn't recall a blessed word. Instead she said the first thing that came into her mind. "I see your taste in transportation hasn't improved."

A smile teased the corners of his lips, but he didn't move so much as a muscle when he replied, "Is there another way to go down here? At least this time I almost made it to the front gate."

He stopped talking and simply stared at her; the thirst that must have built up after pushing the truck even a short distance under the searing midday sun seemed to be quenched as he drank in her appearance. His gaze left no inch of her uncovered, and she felt the oddest sensation of being naked before him. She also found it didn't bother her in the least. That knowledge gave her the strength to start walking again, slowly closing the distance between them.

"Why don't you leave everything here and I'll send down one of the carts to bring you up."

"I guess you didn't learn much either, huh?" The teasing edge was still there as he moved around to the side of the truck and lifted a large duffel bag and the ever-present silver case and set them on the ground at his feet. She simply stared back at him, and he added, "I'll leave the truck, but—"

"No one touches my equipment," she finished. "I learned more than you think."

"Good; I was banking on that."

April stopped a few feet away, the change in his tone making her feel suddenly vulnerable and unsure. She knew what she wanted. She wanted Jack. But until she knew what he wanted, she had to keep her barriers intact. If she let him past them this time, she wouldn't survive his leaving again. "What are you doing here?"

"Officially? I'm here to do an in-depth study of the local Indian cultures and their descent from power in modern times."

April's eyes widened. "That's a pretty big task. Isn't that a bit outside of your usual field?"

"Maybe. But I became fascinated by the culture while I was here and in Oaxaca, so I did a little research and managed to convince a good friend of mine who happens to owe me a favor or two that this would be a worthwhile project."

April couldn't contain her smile. "Leave it to Jack Tango to charm the publishing industry into backing him on a project no one else has been able to get more than an occasional pittance of a grant for in decades."

Jack's slight smile disappeared at her teasing tone. "What if I told you I was funding this little expedition out-of-pocket."

Wary, April studied his face for clues as to where this was leading, but she couldn't read much in his closed expression. "I'd say that it was admirable, and that if anyone could make such a time-consuming project pay off it would be you."

"Yes, it may be *very* time-consuming. And I have every intention of making it 'pay off.'" Jack took a step closer to her, his eyes gazing so intently into hers she felt a physical pull. "Now that we've covered the unimportant stuff, would you like to know the unofficial reason I'm here?"

Overwhelmed by the sudden fear that his reason wouldn't be the one she so desperately needed to hear, she resorted to a brittle laugh and a toss-away line. "You want a cold beer, a shower, and two days of uninterrupted sleep?"

"Those things are on the list. But not at the top."

"What . . ." Her voice faded to a hoarse whisper as Jack closed the remaining distance between them. "What's at the top of the list?"

"You. Under me. Preferably on a bed. For hours. Or for as long as it takes to make you understand that I am here to stay. That I'm yours, have been yours since the day you put your hand on my arm and offered to help me." Jack reached out and traced a callused finger down the side of her face. "Do you still want me, *mi tesoro*?"

The burning sensation that had begun when he'd first said "you" gathered strength until her eyes watered and a tear slid from the corner of each eye. "Are you sure, Jack? This is what you want?"

"More than anything else in my life." Without touching any other part of her, he leaned down and kissed the two tears gently off of her cheeks. "I love you, April Marie Morgan de la Torre."

Choking on a sob, April threw her arms around his neck and instantly found herself locked in a tight embrace created by the steel of his arms around her. "I know I should have trusted you, agreed to let you help—"

"Shhh. I realize now that it was something you had to work out for yourself." He lifted her chin until their gazes met. "I won't lie and say it didn't hurt. It hurt like hell."

"Is that why you left the folder?"

"I thought I could walk away from it all; you, the story, all of it. But I was wrong. I hadn't realized how much I wanted you to decide that I—we—were worth fighting for."

Wiping the tears from her cheeks, she said, "You were right about coming back. It was your belief in me as much as the information in that folder that made it possible for me to do what I did."

"Whatever the reason, I'm just glad you did. Do you know how proud I was of you for going back? The guts it took to take a stand without any backup? You were incredible, so poised . . ."

"You saw the interview?" she asked, thrilled that he'd been proud of her. Then something in his expression, a subtle shift of his eyes, made her pause. And suddenly, understanding rushed in. "You *were* there. That day, on the set."

"I was."

"I knew it! You'll probably think this is nuts, but I could feel you. I swore I actually saw you at one point, but . . ."

"It's not nuts. You looked straight at me. I almost had heart failure from the effect you had on me."

April suddenly pulled his arms. Jack loosened his grip somewhat, but didn't let her go. "Uh-uh. You have a doubt, you ask me. I will always answer you honestly."

"When I didn't hear from you, I thought it—we—were over. Why didn't you try to see me? Talk to me?"

"For the same reason I let you walk out of the bungalow that day. When I found out about the potential story, I was surprised at how badly I needed to follow through on it. After Oaxaca, I really thought that part of my life was over. On the trip back to the Cove, I had already started thinking of a way to make this Indian-story project work. But when I felt that old urge consume me, I knew I had no right to make any claims on you, or ask anything of you until I worked it out."

"Did you work on the story when you got back to L.A.?"

"Day and night. It became an obsession to me." Jack folded her back against his chest. "I had to make sure the bastard paid, even if it was only with his career. I wanted to make damn sure that if your name was involved this time around, you wouldn't be burned again."

"How could I *not* be involved . . ." April jerked her head up. "*You* found Frannie, didn't you? You got her to come forward."

"I found her, but I was planning on doing the whole interview through the papers, not television. As a matter of fact, I'd just located her the night before your interview."

"How did you find out—"

"Your father called me," he broke in gently. "He tracked me down in my office in L.A., said he thought I should know." Jack traced her jawline with his finger. "You told him about me?"

"I didn't ask him to call you, if that's what you mean."

"No, I knew you had no idea. You two mending fences okay? You glad you took the first step?"

"Well, the fence was destroyed pretty thoroughly, so it will take a while to rebuild, but we're trying. He's coming down in a few weeks. As a matter of fact, I was just on my way to the gate to get some newspapers he sent down."

"You still want to do that?"

"No, I think I've suddenly lost all interest in what they have to say."

The teasing light entered his eyes again and April felt her eyes well up once more. She'd thought she'd seen that look for the last time.

"Here I am dying in the heat and you're turning into a one-woman waterworks," he teased.

"I know it's silly, it's just . . ." She tried to get herself under control but found the task finally beyond her. "I never thought I'd see you again and . . . I love you, Jack Tango. I love you."

"Say that again. And again." But he couldn't wait. He lowered his mouth to hers, his kiss hot and hard. He kissed her relentlessly, pouring into it all the frustration and fear, all the hope and love he'd held in check waiting to hear those three words. He wanted to push his tongue deeper inside her sweet mouth, to absorb the taste and feel of her until it was a permanent part of his own essence.

She responded instantly and the world exploded. Jack held her tightly against his chest and stepped back until he could lean against the side of the truck. He pulled her between his legs, reveling in the feel of her slender hips cradling his hardness. He pulled the pins from her hair and tossed them over his head into the open bed of the truck, then dug his hands under the swirling mass to gently grip her neck. Turning her face up to his, he proceeded to cover every inch of her face with his kisses.

"You say you've lost interest in reading," he rasped against her neck. "Anything else I can interest you in?"

April smiled, breathing in the scent of his hair, gripping his shoulders tighter as he nipped at her earlobes and growled seductively in her ears. "Actually, the bed of that truck is looking pretty good right about now."

Jack's head jerked back in surprise, then he grinned and let out a deep laugh. "I love it when you're direct."

His teasing was contagious, and April wanted to steep herself in his special brand of loving that she'd missed so intensely. "I also know," she continued as if he hadn't spoken, giving him the best CEO voice she could muster under the circumstances, "that you have this rather conventional taste for soft beds and clean sheets."

"Is that an invitation?"

"Your bungalow or mine?"

Jack's eyes lost a bit of their twinkle and his voice became earnest. "Did you mean what you said earlier?"

"I love you, Jack. I want you here as long as you're willing to stay."

"Then I won't be needing a bungalow." At her raised eyebrow, he relented and smiled. "That is, unless yours isn't big enough to hold all my equipment."

April smiled, then laughed as a feeling of pure light swept through her. "Is that a proposal?"

"Not a well-said one, I'm afraid, but yes, it was." Jack looked down at her face, rocked again by all that love shining in them—all for him. "Standing in that studio, listening to you—the courage it took . . . your voice, your laughter. I knew then that my need to do the story came from loving you, from the uncontrollable need to right the wrong in your life. I don't need that part of my life anymore to make me whole. What I need is you. Marry me, April."

April's smile was tremulous through her tears. Her heart so full she could barely speak, she managed, "On one condition."

Jack groaned and tugged her more tightly against the growing bulge in his jeans. "Name it."

"We get someone else to take the pictures."

Jack laughed hard as he hugged April closer. "Deal." He looked into her eyes. "I love you, you know."

"Yeah," she answered, suddenly serious. "I know."

Jack kissed her again, fiercely, gently, thoroughly, until he knew if he didn't stop he'd take her right there on the pavement. He meant to let her go, but found he had to do it in stages. Pressing her shoulders back, but keeping her thighs trapped between his, he said, "In that case, would you help me?"

April smiled. "If it means we get to go back to the Cove, I'll agree to anything."

"I was counting on that." Jack reluctantly shifted out from between her and the truck and reached down for his bags. Without comment, he handed her the silver case. "Carry this for me?"

"It must be love if you're trusting me with your equipment," she shot back as she took the case from his hand.

Jack chuckled as he hoisted the duffel onto his back, then leaned into the truck to get another smaller gym bag. He turned back to her with a smile and April felt her heart go right through her feet. "Play your cards right, *Señorita* CEO, and I'll even let you play with my telephoto lens."

April lifted up on tiptoes and kissed him on the lips and whispered, "I can hardly wait to see what develops."

THE EDITOR'S CORNER

Next month, LOVESWEPT is proud to present **CONQUERING HEROES,** six men who know what they want and won't stop until they get it. Just when summer is really heating up, our six wonderful romances sizzle with bold seduction and daring promises of passion. You'll meet the heroes of your wildest fantasies who will risk everything in pursuit of the women they desire, and like our heroines, you'll learn that surrender comes easily when love conquers all.

The ever-popular Leanne Banks gives us the story of another member of the Pendleton family in **PLAYING WITH DYNAMITE,** LOVESWEPT #696. Brick Pendleton is stunned when Lisa Ransom makes love to him like a wild woman, then sends him away! He cares for her as he never has another woman, but he just can't give her the promise that she insists is her dearest dream. Lisa tries to forget him, ignore him, but he's gotten under her skin, claiming her with every caress of his mouth and hands. The fierce demolition expert knows everything about tearing things down, but rebuilding Lisa's trust means fighting old demons—and confessing fear. **PLAYING WITH DYNAMITE** is another explosive winner from Leanne.

CAPTAIN'S ORDERS, LOVESWEPT #697, is the newest sizzling romance from Susan Connell, with a hero you'll be more than happy to obey. When marina captain Rick Parrish gets home from vacation, the last thing he expects to find is his favorite hang-out turned into a fancy restaurant by Bryn Madison. The willowy redhead redesigning her grandfather's bar infuriates him with her plan to sell the jukebox and get rid of the parrot, but she stirs long-forgotten needs and touches him in dark and lonely places. Fascinated by the arrogant and impossibly handsome man who fights to hide the passion inside him, Bryn aches to unleash it. This determined angel has the power to heal his sorrow and capture his soul, but Rick has to face his ghosts before he can make her his forever. This heart-stopping romance is what you've come to expect from Susan Connell.

It's another powerful story of triumph from Judy Gill in **LOVING VOICES**, LOVESWEPT #698. Ken Ransom considers his life over, cursing the accident that has taken his sight, but when a velvety angel voice on the telephone entices him to listen and talk, he feels like a man again—and aches to know the woman whose warmth has lit a fire in his soul. Ingrid Bjornson makes him laugh, and makes him long to stroke her until she moans with pleasure, but he needs to persuade her to meet him face-to-face. Ingrid fears revealing her own lonely secret to the man whose courage is greater than her own, but he dares her to be reckless, to let him court her, cherish her, and awaken her deepest yearnings. Ken can't believe he's found the woman destined to fill his heart just when he has nothing to offer her, but now they must confront the pain that has drawn them together. Judy Gill will have you laughing and crying with this terrific love story.

Linda Warren invites you to get **DOWN AND DIRTY**, LOVESWEPT #699. When Jack Gibraltar refuses to help archeology professor Catherine Moore find her missing aunt, he doesn't expect her to trespass on his turf, looking for information in the seedy Mexican bar! He admires her persistence, but she is going to ruin a perfectly good con if she keeps asking questions . . . not to mention drive him crazy wondering what she'll taste like when he kisses her. When they are forced to play lovers to elude their pursuers, they pretend it's only a game—until he claims her mouth with sweet, savage need. Now she has to show her sexy outlaw that loving him is the adventure she craves most. **DOWN AND DIRTY** is Linda Warren at her best.

Jan Hudson's conquering hero is **ONE TOUGH TEXAN**, LOVESWEPT #700. Need Chisholm doesn't think his day could possibly get worse, but when a nearly naked woman appears in the doorway of his Ace in the Hole saloon, he cheers right up! On a scale of one to ten, Kate Miller is a twenty, with hair the color of a dark palomino and eyes that hold secrets worth uncovering, but before he can court her, he has to keep her from running away! With his rakish eye patch and desperado mustache, Need looks tough, dangerous, and utterly masculine, but Kate has never met a man who makes her feel safer—or wilder. Unwilling to endanger the man she loves, yet desperate to stop hiding from her shadowy past, she must find a way to trust the hero who'll follow her anywhere. **ONE TOUGH TEXAN** is vintage Jan Hudson.

And last, but never least, is **A BABY FOR DAISY**, LOVESWEPT #701, from Fayrene Preston. When Daisy Huntington suggests they make a baby together, Ben McGuire gazes at her with enough intensity to strip the varnish from the nightclub bar! Regretting her impulsive words almost immediately, Daisy wonders if the man might just be worth the challenge. But when she finds an abandoned baby in her car minutes later, then quickly realizes that several dangerous men are searching for the child, Ben becomes her only hope for escape! Something in his cool gray eyes makes her trust him—and the electricity between them is too delicious to deny. He wants her from the moment he sees her, hungers to touch her everywhere, but he has to convince her that what they have will endure. Fayrene has done it again with a romance you'll never forget.

Happy reading,

With warmest wishes,

Nita Taublib

Nita Taublib

Associate Publisher

P.S. There are exciting things happening here at Loveswept! Stay tuned for our gorgeous new look starting with our August 1994 books—on sale in July. More details to come next month.

P.P.S. Don't miss the exciting women's novels from Bantam that are coming your way in July—**MISTRESS** is the newest hardcover from *New York Times* best-selling author Amanda Quick; **WILDEST DREAMS,** by best-selling author Rosanne Bittner, is the epic, romantic saga of a young beauty and a rugged ex-soldier with the courage to face hardship and deprivation for the sake of their dreams; **DANGEROUS TO LOVE,** by award-winning Elizabeth Thornton, is a spectacular historical romance brimming with passion, humor, and adventure; **AMAZON LILY,** by Theresa Weir, is the classic love story in the best-selling tradition of *Romancing the Stone* that sizzles with passionate romance and adventure as deadly as the uncharted heart of the Amazon. We'll be giving you a sneak peek at these terrific books in next month's LOVESWEPTs. And immediately following this page look for a preview of the exciting romances from Bantam that are *available now*!

Don't miss these extraordinary books by
your favorite Bantam authors

On sale in May:

DARK JOURNEY
by Sandra Canfield

SOMETHING BORROWED, SOMETHING BLUE
by Jillian Karr

THE MOON RIDER
by Virginia Lynn

DARK JOURNEY
by Sandra Canfield

*From the day Anna Ramey moved to Cook's Bay, Maine,
with her dying husband—to the end of the summer when
she discovers the price of forbidden passion in another
man's arms, DARK JOURNEY is nothing less than
electrifying.* Affaire de Coeur *has already praised it as
"emotionally moving and thoroughly fascinating," and*
Rendezvous *calls it "A masterful work."*

Here is a look at this powerful novel . . .

"Jack and I haven't been lovers for years," Anna
said, unable to believe she was being so frank. She'd
never made this admission to anyone before. She
blamed the numbness, which in part was culpable,
but she also knew that the man sitting beside her
had a way of making her want to share her thoughts
and feelings.

Her statement in no way surprised Sloan. He'd
suspected Jack's impotence was the reason there
had been no houseful of children. He further suspected that the topic of discussion had something
to do with what was troubling Anna, but he let her
find her own way of telling him that.

"As time went on, I adjusted to that fact," Anna
said finally. She thought of her lonely bed and of

more lonely nights than she could count, and added, "One adjusts to what one has to."

Again Sloan said nothing, though he could painfully imagine the price she'd paid.

"I learned to live with celibacy," Anna said. "What I couldn't learn to live with was . . ."

Her voice faltered. The numbness that had claimed her partially receded, allowing a glimpse of her earlier anger to return.

Sloan saw the flash of anger. She was feeling, which was far healthier than not feeling, but again she was paying a dear price.

"What couldn't you live with, Anna?"

The query came so softly, so sweetly, that Anna had no choice but to respond. But, then, it would have taken little persuasion, for she wanted—no, needed!—to tell this man just how much she was hurting.

"All I wanted was an occasional touch, a hug, someone to hold my hand, some contact!" She had willed her voice to sound normal, but the anger had a will of its own. On some level she acknowledged that the anger felt good. "He won't touch me, and he won't let me touch him!"

Though a part of Sloan wanted to deck Jack Ramey for his insensitivity, another part of him understood. How could a man remember what it was like to make love to this woman, then touch her knowing that the touch must be limited because of his incapability?

"I reached for his hand, and he pulled it away." Anna's voice thickened. "Even when I begged him, he wouldn't let me touch him."

Sloan heard the hurt, the desolation of spirit, that lay behind her anger. No matter the circumstances, he couldn't imagine any man not responding to this woman's need. He couldn't imagine any man having the option. He himself had spent the better part of the morning trying to forget the gentle touch of her hand, and here she was pleading with her husband for what he—Sloan—would die to give her.

A part of Anna wanted to show Sloan the note crumpled in her pants pocket, but another part couldn't bring herself to do it. She couldn't believe that Jack was serious about wishing for death. He was depressed. Nothing more.

"What can I do to ease your pain?" Sloan asked, again so softly that his voice, like a log-fed fire, warmed Anna.

Take my hand. The words whispered in Anna's head, in her heart. They seemed as natural as the currents, the tides of the ocean, yet they shouldn't have.

Let me take your hand, Sloan thought, admitting that maybe his pain would be eased by that act. For pain was exactly what he felt at being near her and not being able to touch her. Dear God, when had touching her become so important? Ever since that morning's silken memories, came the reply.

What would he do if I took his hand?
What would she do if I took her hand?

The questions didn't wait for answers. As though each had no say in the matter, as though it had been ordained from the start, Sloan reached for Anna's hand even as she reached for his.

A hundred recognitions scrambled through two minds: warmth, Anna's softness, Sloan's strength, the smallness of Anna's hand, the largeness of Sloan's, the way Anna's fingers entwined with his as though clinging to him for dear life, the way Sloan's fingers tightened about hers as though he'd fight to the death to defend her.

What would it feel like to thread his fingers through her golden hair?

What would it feel like to palm his stubble-shaded cheek?

What would it feel like to trace the delicate curve of her neck?

What would it feel like to graze his lips with her fingertips?

Innocently, guiltily, Sloan's gaze met Anna's. They stared—at each other, at the truth boldly staring back at them.

With her wedding band glinting an ugly accusation, Anna slowly pulled her hand from Sloan's. She said nothing, though her fractured breath spoke volumes.

Sloan's breath was no steadier when he said, "I swear I never meant for this to happen."

Anna stood, Sloan stood, the world spun wildly. Anna took a step backward as though by doing so she could outdistance what she was feeling.

Sloan saw flight in her eyes. "Anna, wait. Let's talk."

But Anna didn't. She took another step, then another, and then, after one last look in Sloan's eyes, she turned and raced from the beach.

"Anna, please . . . Anna . . . *Ann-nna!*"

SOMETHING BORROWED, SOMETHING BLUE

by

Jillian Karr

When the "Comtesse" Monique D'Arcy decides to feature four special weddings on the pages of her floundering *Perfect Bride* magazine, the brides find themselves on a collision course of violent passions and dangerous desires.

The T.V. movie rights for this stunning novel have already been optioned to CBS.

The intercom buzzed, braying intrusively into the early morning silence of the office.

Standing by the window, looking down at the sea of umbrellas bobbing far below, Monique D'Arcy took another sip of her coffee, ignoring the insistent drone, her secretary's attempt to draw her into the formal start of this workday. Not yet, Linda. The Sinutab hasn't kicked in. What the hell could be so important at seven-thirty in the morning?

She closed her eyes and pressed the coffee mug into the hollow between her brows, letting the warmth seep into her aching sinuses. The intercom buzzed on, relentless, five staccato blasts that reverberated through Monique's head like a jackhammer.

"Dammit."

She tossed the fat, just-published June issue of *Perfect Bride* and a stack of next month's galleys aside to unearth the intercom buried somewhere on her marble desk. She pressed the button resignedly. "You win, Linda. What's up?"

"Hurricane warning."

"*What?*" Monique spun back toward the window and scanned the dull pewter skyline marred with rain clouds. Manhattan was getting soaked in a May downpour and her window shimmered with delicate crystal droplets, but no wind buffeted the panes. "Linda, what are you talking . . ."

"Shanna Ives," Linda hissed. "She's on her way up. Thought you'd like to know."

Adrenaline pumped into her brain, surging past the sinus headache as Monique dove into her fight or flee mode. She started pacing, her Maud Frizon heels digging into the plush vanilla carpet. Shanna was the last person in the world she wanted to tangle with this morning. She was still trying to come to grips with the June issue, with all that had happened. As she set the mug down amid the organized clutter of her desk, she realized her hands were shaking. Get a grip. Don't let that bitch get the better of you. *Oh, God, this is the last thing I need today.*

Her glance fell on the radiant faces of the three brides smiling out at her from the open pages of the magazine, faces that had haunted her since she'd found the first copies of the June issue in a box beside her desk a scant half hour earlier.

Grief tore at her. Oh, God, only three of us. There were supposed to have been four. There *should* have been four. Her heart cried out for the one who was missing.

This had all been her idea. Four stunning brides, the weddings of the year, showcased in dazzling style. Save the magazine, save my ass, make Richard happy. All of us famed celebrities—except for one.

Teri. She smiled, thinking of the first time she'd met the pretty little manicurist who'd been so peculiarly reluctant at first to be thrust into the limelight. Most women dreamed of the Cinderella chance she'd been offered, yet Teri had recoiled from it. *But I made it impossible for her to refuse. I never guessed where it would lead, or what it would do to her life.*

And Ana, Hollywood's darling, with that riot of red curls framing a delicate face, exuding sexy abandon. Monique had found Ana perhaps the most vulnerable and private of them all. *Poor, beautiful Ana, with her sad, ugly secrets—I never dreamed anyone could have as much to hide as I do.*

And then there was Eve—lovely, tigerish Eve, Monique's closest friend in the world, the once-lanky, unsure teenage beauty she had discovered and catapulted to international supermodel fame. *All I asked was one little favor . . .*

And me, Monique reflected with a bittersweet smile, staring at her own glamorous image alongside the other two brides. Unconsciously, she twisted the two-and-a-half-carat diamond on her finger. Monique D'Arcy, the Comtesse de Chevalier. *If only they knew the truth.*

Shanna Ives would be bursting through her door any minute, breathing fire. But Monique couldn't stop thinking about the three women whose lives had become so bound up with her own during the past months. Teri, Ana, Eve—all on the brink of living happily ever after with the men they loved . . .

For one of them the dream had turned into a nightmare. *You never know what life will spring on you*, Monique thought, sinking into her chair as the rain pelted more fiercely against the window. *You just never know. Not one of us could have guessed what would happen.*

She hadn't, that long-ago dawn when she'd first conceived the plan for salvaging the magazine, her job, and her future with Richard. Her brilliant plan. She'd had no idea of what she was getting all of them into. . . .

THE MOON RIDER

by VIRGINIA LYNN

bestselling author of
IN A ROGUE'S ARMS

"Lynn's novels shine with lively adventures,
a special brand of humor
and sizzling romance."
—*Romantic Times*

*When a notorious highwayman accosted Rhianna and
her father on a lonely country road, the evening ended
in tragedy. Now, desperate for the funds to care for her
bedridden father, Rhianna has hit upon an ingenious
scheme: she too will take up a sword—and let the heart-
less highwayman take the blame for her robberies. But
in the blackness of the night the Moon Rider waits, and
soon this reckless beauty will find herself at his mercy,
in his arms, and in the thrall of his raging passion.*

"Stand and deliver," she heard the highwayman
say as the coach door was jerked open. Rhianna
gasped at the stark white apparition.

Keswick had not exaggerated. The highwayman
was swathed in white from head to foot, and she
thought at once of the childhood tales of ghosts
that had made her shiver with delicious dread.

There was nothing delicious about this apparition.

A silk mask of snow-white was over his face, dark eyes seeming to burn like banked fires beneath the material. Only his mouth was partially visible, and he was repeating the order to stand and deliver. He stepped closer to the coach, his voice rough and impatient.

Llewellyn leaned forward into the light, and the masked highwayman checked his forward movement.

"We have no valuables," her father said boldly. Lantern light glittered along the slender length of the cane sword he held in one hand. "I demand that you go your own way and leave us in peace."

"Don't be a fool," the Moon Rider said harshly. "Put away your weapon, sir."

"I have never yielded to a coward, and only cowards hide behind a mask, you bloody knave." He gave a thrust of his sword. There was a loud clang of metal and the whisk of steel on steel before Llewellyn's sword went flying through the air.

For a moment, Rhianna thought the highwayman intended to run her father through with his drawn sword. Then he lowered it slightly. She studied him, trying to fix his image in her mind so that she could describe him to the sheriff.

A pistol was tucked into the belt he wore around a long coat of white wool. The night wind tugged at a cape billowing behind him. Boots of white leather fit him to the knee, and his snug breeches were streaked with mud. He should have been a laughable figure, but he exuded such fierce menace that Rhianna could find no jest in what she'd earlier thought an amusing hoax.

"Give me one reason why I should not kill you on the spot," the Moon Rider said softly.

Rhianna shivered. "Please sir—" Her voice quivered and she paused to steady it. "Please—my father means no harm. Let us pass."

"One must pay the toll to pass this road tonight, my lovely lady." He stepped closer, and Rhianna was reminded of the restless prowl of a panther she'd once seen. "What have you to pay me?"

Despite her father's angry growl, Rhianna quickly unfastened her pearl necklace and held it out. "This. Take it and go. It's all of worth that I have, little though it is."

The Moon Rider laughed softly. "Ah, you underestimate yourself, my lady fair." He reached out and took the necklace from her gloved hand, then grasped her fingers. When her father moved suddenly, he was checked by the pistol cocked and aimed at him.

"Do not be hasty, my friend," the highwayman mocked. "A blast of ball and powder is much messier than the clean slice of a sword. Rest easy. I do not intend to debauch your daughter." He pulled her slightly closer. "Though she is a very tempting morsel, I must admit."

"You swine," Llewellyn choked out. Rhianna was alarmed at his high color. She tugged her hand free of the Moon Rider's grasp.

"You have what you wanted, now go and leave us in peace," she said firmly. For a moment, she thought he would grab her again, but he stepped back.

"My thanks for the necklace."

"Take it to hell with you," Llewellyn snarled. Rhianna put a restraining hand on his arm. The Moon Rider only laughed, however, and reached out for his horse.

Rhianna's eyes widened. She hadn't noticed the horse, but now she saw that it was a magnificent Arabian. Sleek and muscled, the pure white beast was as superb an animal as she'd ever seen and she couldn't help a soft exclamation of admiration.

"Oh! He's beautiful. . . ."

The Moon Rider swung into his saddle and glanced back at her. "I salute your perception, my fair lady."

Rhianna watched, her fear fading as the highwayman swung his horse around and pounded off into the shadows. He was a vivid contrast to the darker shapes of trees and bushes, easily seen until he crested the hill. Then, to her amazement, with the full moon silvering the ground and making it almost shimmer with light, he seemed to vanish. She blinked. It couldn't be. He was a man, not a ghost.

One of the footmen gave a whimper of pure fear. She ignored it as she stared at the crest of the hill, waiting for she didn't know what.

Then she saw him, a faint outline barely visible. He'd paused and was looking back at the coach. Several heartbeats thudded past, then he was gone again, and she couldn't recall later if he'd actually ridden away or somehow just faded into nothing.

OFFICIAL RULES

To enter the sweepstakes below carefully follow all instructions found elsewhere in this offer.

The **Winners Classic** will award prizes with the following approximate maximum values: 1 Grand Prize: $26,500 (or $25,000 cash alternate); 1 First Prize: $3,000; 5 Second Prizes: $400 each; 35 Third Prizes: $100 each; 1,000 Fourth Prizes: $7.50 each. Total maximum retail value of Winners Classic Sweepstakes is $42,500. Some presentations of this sweepstakes may contain individual entry numbers corresponding to one or more of the aforementioned prize levels. To determine the Winners, individual entry numbers will first be compared with the winning numbers preselected by computer. For winning numbers not returned, prizes will be awarded in random drawings from among all eligible entries received. Prize choices may be offered at various levels. If a winner chooses an automobile prize, all license and registration fees, taxes, destination charges and, other expenses not offered herein are the responsibility of the winner. If a winner chooses a trip, travel must be complete within one year from the time the prize is awarded. Minors must be accompanied by an adult. Travel companion(s) must also sign release of liability. Trips are subject to space and departure availability. Certain black-out dates may apply.

The following applies to the sweepstakes named above:

No purchase necessary. You can also enter the sweepstakes by sending your name and address to: P.O. Box 508, Gibbstown, N.J. 08027. Mail each entry separately. Sweepstakes begins 6/1/93. Entries must be received by 12/30/94. Not responsible for lost, late, damaged, misdirected, illegible or postage due mail. Mechanically reproduced entries are not eligible. All entries become property of the sponsor and will not be returned.

Prize Selection/Validations: Selection of winners will be conducted no later than 5:00 PM on January 28, 1995, by an independent judging organization whose decisions are final. Random drawings will be held at 1211 Avenue of the Americas, New York, N.Y. 10036. Entrants need not be present to win. Odds of winning are determined by total number of entries received. Circulation of this sweepstakes is estimated not to exceed 200 million. All prizes are guaranteed to be awarded and delivered to winners. Winners will be notified by mail and may be required to complete an affidavit of eligibility and release of liability which must be returned within 14 days of date on notification or alternate winners will be selected in a random drawing. Any prize notification letter or any prize returned to a participating sponsor, Bantam Doubleday Dell Publishing Group, Inc., its participating divisions or subsidiaries, or the independent judging organization as undeliverable will be awarded to an alternate winner. Prizes are not transferable. No substitution for prizes except as offered or as may be necessary due to unavailability, in which case a prize of equal or greater value will be awarded. Prizes will be awarded approximately 90 days after the drawing. All taxes are the sole responsibility of the winners. Entry constitutes permission (except where prohibited by law) to use winners' names, hometowns, and likenesses for publicity purposes without further or other compensation. Prizes won by minors will be awarded in the name of parent or legal guardian.

Participation: Sweepstakes open to residents of the United States and Canada, except for the province of Quebec. Sweepstakes sponsored by Bantam Doubleday Dell Publishing Group, Inc., (BDD), 1540 Broadway, New York, NY 10036. Versions of this sweepstakes with different graphics and prize choices will be offered in conjunction with various solicitations or promotions by different subsidiaries and divisions of BDD. Where applicable, winners will have their choice of any prize offered at level won. Employees of BDD, its divisions, subsidiaries, advertising agencies, independent judging organization, and their immediate family members are not eligible.

Canadian residents, in order to win, must first correctly answer a time limited arithmetical skill testing question. Void in Puerto Rico, Quebec and wherever prohibited or restricted by law. Subject to all federal, state, local and provincial laws and regulations. For a list of major prize winners (available after 1/29/95): send a self-addressed, stamped envelope entirely separate from your entry to: Sweepstakes Winners, P.O. Box 517, Gibbstown, NJ 08027. Requests must be received by 12/30/94. DO NOT SEND ANY OTHER CORRESPONDENCE TO THIS P.O. BOX.